LOST IN THE SHADOWS

JULIAN BLACKWOOD

Contents

1

Divided / We Stand

I was standing there, next to the surgeon, watching him firmly and carefully cutting along the edges of a wound in the side of someone laying on the operating table before him. A red line of blood, adding to that already released by the wound, was tracing the path of the scalpel as it sliced through flesh. A nurse mopped up the blood to keep the area clean for the surgeon.

The curious thing that hit me was the simple fact that the person on the table was me. I was laying there on the table, but I was also standing at the side watching the events.

A memory flashed before my eyes of the car heading towards me; the headlights were blinding me as they reflected off the rain-soaked road. I heard a squeal of tyres assaulting my ears as the driver tried to avoid the inevitable.

The squeal was replaced with a flat tone from the heart monitor when my senses returned. I was back in the room in time to hear the surgeon ask for everyone to step back as he placed the defibrillator pads onto my chest.

There was a buzz, my body lurched, and nothing changed.

The flat tone was still playing, and a nurse started to pound rhythmically on my chest.

Overtones of "Another One Bites the Dust" played in my mind with the consistency of the beat the nurse was keeping. I fancied myself standing next to Freddie singing along to the music and shaggy haired Brian strumming like there's no tomorrow behind us both.

I saw the surgeon begin another attempt with the defibrillator, and I gently smiled. 'Stop. It's OK. I'm alright,' I said. 'Just let me go.' I knew no one could hear me.

'Clear!' said the surgeon.

Another buzz, another lurch. Still a flat tone.

'They're going to keep trying,' said a man that had appeared next to me.

'Who the hell are you?' I yelled, a little louder than I expected. None of the medics reacted to my outburst, but the man at my side took a step back before he smiled and stepped forward again.

'Henry. Henry Costa, Ghost Buster Extraordinaire. Or I was,' he replied.

'Was?' I blurted. Remembering my manners, I smiled back, taken aback by his polite introduction, I offered a handshake, and I introduced myself in return. 'Jimmy Jones,' I said with a bright smile as we shook hands.

'Well, James,' Henry emphasised my full Sunday name as he released my hand, 'you have a few options. Two real solid ones, and one vague non-choice. Firstly, you can go back. Into your body, shell, meat, whatever you want to call it. I have heard them all. Once there you should, hopefully, live a long, prosperous life.'

I nodded. 'The so-called blue pill.'

'You could give up, and "go to the light". As they say,' Henry continued, unfazed. 'I don't know what's there, I've never seen this mythical light.' His tone was bordering on sarcastic and defeated all at once.

'That sounds like the red pill option,' I said.

'Or,' Henry pressed on ignoring his growing irritation with my interruptions, 'you can take option number three and get stuck for eternity. At least until that good old light appears. Just like me.'

'What's that option? A "brown pill"?'

'What are these pills you keep referring to?' Henry was clearly not impressed with my interruptions.

'How long have you been dead, man? They are references to one of my favourite movies.'

'I died in the early nineteen eighties, Prince Charles had just announced his engagement, I believe, which would be around sixty years ago by my reckoning,' scoffed Henry. 'Besides, I was never much for films and television. Too far-fetched for me. Even some documentaries included some level of fiction, from what I recall.'

I smiled, 'Yeah, I can see where you're coming from with that. And it's not sixty, not yet.'

It then dawned on me that the surgeon was still trying to revive my body, and my attention returned to the action before me.

'I can tell you,' Henry continued, 'you don't want to get stuck like me. It's a literal hell on earth.' Henry was now staring at my body, too. I thought I could see a little envy creeping into his eyes.

'But what am I going back to?'

'Your life.'

The surgeon tried again with the defibrillator. When my body lurched this time, I felt something pulling at me, tugging at me, drawing me back into the 'shell'. At the same time, I could see a light begin to form in the corner of the room.

'Can you see that?' I nudged Henry, pointing to the light.

Henry looked and shrugged. 'I don't. We each see our own future,' he replied

There was a flurry of activity around the operating theatre now. They all seemed excited that there was something positive happening.

The surgeon did his thing again with the defibrillator, and the pull was much stronger this time. In fact, I was moved nearer to the table. At the same time, the light in the corner got brighter. It was almost blinding now.

Time felt like it was speeding up.

Another blast of the defibrillator from the surgeon and I was looking up into his eyes. He didn't register I was looking at him, and I realised that I was actually back in my body, but my body was not awake. I turned to look at Henry, who just smiled and waved. It was almost a salute. He faded from view as he lowered his arm again.

'But,' I started to say. I heard the buzz of the defibrillator once more, and then there was just darkness.

I woke to the gently beeping heart monitor positioned by the side of me. The rhythm was steady and soothing. Slowly, I opened my eyes and saw the lights around me were out. The only light I could use was coming from the screen of the monitor to which I was attached.

The lights of the screen reflected dully off the privacy curtain that had been drawn between my bed and the one next to me.

'Hello?' I croaked into the darkness.

I heard a rustling of papers and a chair scraping along the floor. A moment later, a smiling face appeared around the curtain. 'Mr. Jones, you're awake. It's quite late,' and the nurse checked the watch on her wrist, 'or early. Depending on how you look at it.'

She looked up again, and I noticed how her curly hair bobbed with the motion. Her smile was infectious.

I tried to sit up, and she was by my side in a flash. 'Oh, you shouldn't try to move,' she said as she fussed at my side. 'You're going to open your stitches if you're not careful.'

She came round and fluffed up my pillow a little and smoothed out my blanket.

'Thank you. Where am I?' I asked.

'You're in the Haywood. This is ICU. You've had quite a time. Do you want a drink?'

I nodded, and she poured some water into a cup, which she then gently applied to my lips and helped me to drink.

'There. Well, give me a moment and I'll fetch the doctor.' Again, she smiled her sweet smile, which I could only return, and she was gone.

When the doctor came, I was standing up looking at the monitors, keeping track of my vitals.

'Hi, I'm Jimmy,' I said and held my hand out to greet him.

The doctor rushed straight through me, and I realised with horror that I'd left my body again.

'Mr. Jones. Can you hear me?' said the doctor. I turned to see he was rubbing the breastbone of my rig cage vigorously.

Stepping to the side, I could see that my eyes were open, and I was staring up at the ceiling.

The nice nurse with the curly hair was there too, and she had her finger on my pulse point. 'It's a strong pulse,' she said. They both shook their heads in confusion.

'What the hell is going on here?' exclaimed the doctor as he turned the monitor to him so he could see it clearly.

I stepped back into my body and felt a pull. A moment later, I was blinking from inside my body. 'What's up?' was all I could say.

This shocked the nurse and the doctor. The nurse gasped when I spoke.

'Mr. Jones?' said the doctor. 'My name is Ben Sharpe. I was the surgeon who repaired your injuries. You're one very lucky man. I've never seen injuries like yours and a will to survive like you have. It was touch and go in theatre, but you wouldn't give up. So I didn't either.'

'I remember,' I said. Images of watching the operation to save my life played like a film in my head.

'I'm sorry?' said the nurse.

I felt my face flush, and I flustered, 'The accident. I remember there was a car and it was raining.'

Nurse Curly Hair smiled again. I was beginning to fall in love with that smile.

Behind the nurse was another figure. 'Henry?' I said.

The nurse turned for a second, thinking I was talking to someone behind her, but she couldn't see Henry.

Henry just smiled. 'Good to see you're on the mend,' he said. He could tell I was about to say something, and he shook his head. 'No, they can't see me. I don't know why you can still, but I'm glad that you can. I've missed having a friend.'

2

HOME / AWAY

I'd been in hospital for nearly three weeks, but the day had finally come for me to leave. Nurse Curly Hair, who I had come to learn was really called Chloe, was absent. Thursdays were her day off. I was sad I wouldn't see that beautiful smile again before I went home.

Henry had been buzzing around me like a blue-arsed fly all morning. 'Young James, you must be quite excited about going home.'

I just nodded, no one was waiting for me. My sister hadn't managed to come, she couldn't get time from work or a suitable flight to visit me whilst I was still in hospital. She'd moved to Florida for her job last year, and she was currently organising a massive technology event at a convention centre in Orlando. Initially Suze had called me every day after my accident, and we'd even done a few video calls, but I knew her job was full-on, and that meant we'd not spoken for nearly a week.

Henry had been kindly playing the "concerned family member" role. He could see I was not happy. 'She'll call. Didn't you say that she's running some conference in Orlando? What was it called, "Tech Fest"?' Henry shook his head, I could see he had no idea what that meant. My mobile phone was a marvel to him, and don't get me started on how he went on about how amazing it was to be able to do video calling. He kept quoting Star Trek lines at me and calling me Mr. Spock.

I nodded and then said, 'Yes, a Technology show, computers and stuff like that. Some big names were booked apparently and Suze had been organising it all. You've probably never heard of them though.'

'I've heard of IBM,' Henry said, a little put out.

I was packing my things into a plastic carrier bag and hardly noticed Henry seemed to be a little upset at my assumption. To be honest, I was more concerned with feeling like a homeless man stuffing all his worldly goods into a tatty old plastic bag.

It felt quite sad, if I'm honest. No one was here, physically, for me right now, no one here to take me home, and no one was waiting for me at home either.

Outside the hospital I headed for the line of taxis I'd seen from my hospital window for the last week and a half. There was a black cab waiting, the driver was reading a paper. The headline I barely paid attention to read "Explosion Toll Now 300".

'Hi, can you take me to Cranden Road, Millbrook?' I said to the driver. He nodded and I climbed in to the back seat.

'Do you mind if I keep the radio on?' the driver asked.

I shrugged as I settled into my seat. The radio was playing the latest songs as we set off and I tuned out a little. I thought the ride itself was comfortable and I felt myself dozing off almost as soon as we started moving.

Some time into the trip, the news broadcast began. I was barely listening, but the report on the state of some explosion in the US half caught my attention. From what I heard, there were many casualties. Unfortunately, I couldn't really concentrate on the story, my tired brain longed for sleep. The news continued into a report of some British political party member doing what all politicians do, and it concluded with a round up of local football. I didn't listen very closely to the details.

'What's this about an explosion?' I asked.

The driver was taken by surprise that I'd spoken. 'Yeah, something big over in The States. I've not really kept up with it to be honest. Lots of dead though, I hear.'

'Sounds bad.' It was the only response I could muster given the driver wasn't forthcoming with many details.

'Where on Cranden?'

I hadn't realised we were so close to home. 'Oh, here's perfect,' I said, suddenly becoming wide awake. My faded green door was visible across the road.

'That's seven quid, mate.'

I dug out a ten pound note from my pocket and handed it over. 'Keep the change.'

The driver smiled and bid me a good day as I exited the taxi.

With my bag of things in my hand, I crossed over as the taxi pulled a u-turn behind me. There was no one around, it was a quiet afternoon so I was shocked to hear someone call out to me.

'Hey, Jim,' came the familiar voice of Mrs. Banwell, the kind old lady from next door. Mrs. Banwell was standing at the end of her drive. Images of the delicious cookies she always made for me came to mind.

I was about to answer with a friendly "hello" when I remembered I'd been to her funeral two years ago. I stopped dead in my tracks.

'Mrs. Banwell?'

She smiled, surprised I'd spoken to her. I waved; all I could do was mimic her gesture.

Without another word, I carried on, fumbling for my front door key and I rushed inside when I'd opened the door. Henry was there to greet me with a smile and open arms.

'Welcome home,' he said. 'Now, James, I strongly suggest you take a seat and rest. Have a nap even. Tomorrow is when you can do whatever it is you want to do.'

All I could do was nod again. I'd seen another ghost, and that disturbed me. At the hospital, there were more ghosts, not just Henry. However, most of the others had kept to themselves, only a small contingent had even waved, smiled or looked my way.

Initially, I'd put the whole ghost thing, even Henry, down to the trauma and medications I was on, and the anaesthesia. But seeing the others, and Mrs. Banwell just now, I was starting to think I was being punished for something.

I was worn out, exhausted, and I decided to veg out in front of the TV. I basically flopped into my favourite chair and reached for the remote.

The first thing I saw was the news from the BBC. The lead story was of this explosion in the US. There was a young man with a heavy southern accent reporting to the studio in the UK. 'We're on day three now of the rescue attempt. All the tech companies involved in the conference have sent volunteers.'

At the mention of the word "conference" all thoughts of sleep vanished.

'Where is this?' I said to the empty room. Henry had done his vanishing trick and was no where to be seen.

I continued to watch and listen as a dawning horror crept over me. 'Henry, where have you gone?'

The camera panned over the scene of devastation and I saw broken, or charred signs from all the major tech companies. Fire and rescue crews were crawling over the wreckage like ants.

I then saw the sign, or at least half of it, for the name of the conference centre. It was the one my sister, Suze, had told me was the location for her technology conference.

'Henry!' I shouted.

3

—·—

Out / Of Body

In a burst of movement I stood up and headed for the stairs to pack a bag and get my passport. Henry had still not made an appearance, which I found slightly odd. He usually arrived when I spoke his name.

At the bottom of the stairs everything went black and I felt my knees buckle. Standing up again, I shook my head to clear my thoughts. I thought I'd simply gone a little dizzy because I'd stood up too quickly; something I have always suffered from.

However, when I looked back to the armchair I saw my body still sitting there looking vacant and a little dazed. In horror I looked down at my hands and feet. They were there, as expected, but something was not right. I could feel my face too, and my hair. It hurt when I tried to pull a little on my cheek. This was really happening, but I was also sat down a few feet away.

Examining my hand a little closer, I could see that I was slightly translucent. I could see the print of the carpet through my feet.

'Henry! Where are you? I need some help here,' I shouted. No response again.

With no other action available, I reached out an arm towards my body. It reacted. The face turned to me and we locked eyes. There was a sparkle, and they looked deeply into, well, my eyes. It was a strange experience. I blinked, and so did the physical version.

Can you speak? I thought.

My body shook its head.

I recoiled away a little. My body could hear my thoughts. Stand up, I commanded in my head.

My physical self complied.

'Henry! How do I get back into my body?'

'It is a puzzling one. Certainly,' said Henry from behind me.

I jumped in fright, and partially passed through the wall between the living room and the kitchen.

There was a pull on my arm and then I was back in the living room. My body self had grabbed my ghostly arm and pulled me back through the wall.

'Thanks,' I said. My body just nodded.

'How are you controlling it?' asked Henry.

'By thinking it, I think. I had the thought just then of "help", and my physical body here grabbed me,' I said.

'Re-joining may be trickier,' said Henry. 'The first time you were pulled back into your body was thanks to the treatment you were getting during surgery.'

The memory of the defibrillator jumped to my mind. 'So, you're saying I've got to lick a battery or something?' I laughed as I spoke, and my body joined in silently.

Then we both looked at each other, Body and me. Screwdriver, was the only thought I had. Body understood with another nod and immediately set off.

I smiled to Henry with a wink and then followed Body. Henry came too, a curious look on his face.

Body had already found a screwdriver in the junk drawer in the kitchen and was heading for a plug socket next to where the kettle was plugged in. Before body began to remove the cover, Henry gently grabbed my arm.

'I don't think this is a wise action,' Henry was saying, but before he could finish Body had removed one of the screws and was working on the other. With no further objections, Body continued removing the other screw and then the cover itself. Body looked at me with a careful stare and then he touched the live terminal with the screwdriver end.

There was a flash, a bang, and everything went black for me again.

A while later, I had no idea how long, I woke with a whole drum section playing a raucous tune in my head. I was back in Body, and we were both me again.

'Remind me to try the battery licking thing next time.' I rubbed the back of my head and my neck.

'You were thrown a couple of feet by the reaction. I think your electrician may well be upset with you now,' said Henry.

Outside the kitchen window it was starting to get dark. 'How long?'

'A few hours, that is certain.' Henry shrugged.

I reached for the light switch, but resisted flicking it. 'I'll have a look at the fuse box.'

Henry was a little bemused by modern life once again. He followed me to my downstairs toilet near the front door. I chuckled as I saw his reaction.

'How many toilets does one need inside?' he asked.

Recalling my grandmother's house with only one outdoor toilet at the end of the back yard, I laughed. 'This isn't the seventies now you know.'

I reached for the fuse box and flipped the mains back on. There was a familiar buzz of appliances reactivating, and Henry was looking about with an I'm impressed expression.

'Now to pack,' I said.

'You're taking a trip?' Henry asked.

'I sure am. I'm off to find Suze.'

It took me an hour to pack, find my passport and verify the details of my US travel visa. It had only been around six months since I went visiting Suze, the weekend we'd spent in Disney sprang to mind, so I would have no issues and I would be able to go almost immediately. That is, assuming I could get a flight.

A flight tracking web site I was looking at in the taxi on the way to the airport told me that there was a flight to New York later today and I had just enough time to get to the airport and check-in. I bought the last seat via the site and arrived with a few minutes to spare.

Aboard the plane, sitting in an expensive business class seat, I let out a heavy sigh. I knew that once I was in JFK airport I'd have to book on another flight to Orlando. This trip was about to make a huge dent in my finances.

'This must have cost you a pretty penny or two,' said Henry standing next to me.

I nodded. 'It was the last seat,' I hissed trying not to look like I was talking to myself. The cabin staff were all concentrating on preparing for the flight, and none of the other passengers were paying any attention to anything but their own little worlds.

The journey to JFK was as dull and as boring as I remember from the last time. Thankfully, I was able to book my follow-on flight by connecting to the WiFi on the plane, and that flight was due to depart around an hour after we landed.

Security at JFK was as intense as I remember, but not as bad as it could have been if this was my destination. The seat I had on the second plane was not as nice, I was just glad it wasn't as long a flight as the one from the UK.

I settled in and allowed my mind to drift to memories of Suze and me growing up. With being twins, we did almost everything together and memories of the birthday party we had the week before she flew off to her new adventure replayed over and over.

The memories helped me to drift off to sleep and influenced my dreams heavily.

After more than twelve hours of travelling, I stepped out of Orlando International into a sweltering afternoon heat.

A line of taxis was waiting outside and I flagged one down. I asked the driver to take me to Suze's apartment block, I was hoping to find her there, or at least some sign of her. I was about to get into the front passenger seat when I spotted a ghost sitting there. The stern expression on her face made me move to the back door instead.

On the journey the driver was telling me all about the recent explosion, how it was impacting all taxis, and how the increased journey times were making prices higher. It was just small-talk and I sensed he was a little on the nervous side when I had hardly responded to comments about what was going on. After twenty minutes the driver eventually asked, 'What brings you here to the beautiful city of Orlando?'

'My sister was working at the place where the explosion happened. I need to find out if she is okay.'

When I mentioned why I wanted to go there, the driver's face paled. But he then nodded with a friendly, sympathetic smile. 'Sure, my friend. Please let me help you.'

I still hadn't mentioned the woman ghost sitting in the front passenger seat, she kept looking between myself and the driver. There was a clear resemblance between the two, and I mouthed to her silently asking if the driver was her son. She smiled and nodded, and her expression towards me softened.

On our journey to Suze's, I saw other ghosts too. Thankfully not that many. One or two I saw were clearly murdered; the wounds on them were significant. A few others I saw had no obvious cause of death, but were still hanging around. All of these ghosts were staying close to a living person. Effectively, these ghosts were haunting these people. It was mildly disturbing to see.

At the apartment block, a nice looking eleven storey building, I paid the driver and smiled at his mother. Outside, there was the ghost of a little girl standing there playing with a doll she held. When she looked at me I smiled, and she smiled back before disappearing through the wall into the apartment building.

Suze had given me a key when I came visiting, so I was able to access the building, and possibly her apartment too, if I needed. Her job required her to work long hours at times and without the key, I would be either stuck inside or outside all day waiting for her to come home.

'She looks like a disturbed soul,' said Henry at my side while I was fishing out the key.

'Really? How do you tell?' I asked, quietly as we walked to the lifts inside; Suze's apartment was on the eighth floor.

'The dark stain around her. Tells me she was murdered. It is hard to look at sometimes,' continued Henry.

I knew exactly what he meant about the stain. It hurt my eyes a little to look at her. 'One day, we need to talk about this,' I pointed to myself and the general area. Henry just nodded.

When we reached Suze's I knocked on the door. I didn't want to just walk in on her. 'Suze, it's me, Jimmy,' I said through the door.

There was no answer so I knocked again. The neighbour from across the hall came out at my second knock.

'She ain't in,' said the man. 'Not seen her in a few days.'

'Thanks,' I said. 'I was just checking, I didn't want to burst in on her if she was busy.' I then showed him the key and the man shrugged and went back into his apartment.

In a moment, I was inside the apartment and I dropped my bag onto the bed in the spare bedroom I'd used last time I was here.

'Where are we going?' asked Henry when he saw I was heading straight back out.

'The nearest police precinct, I thought I would start there. I doubt I'll get near to the site of the explosion.'

I saw the little girl again when we returned to street level and she just giggled and ran away. There were, thankfully, no other ghosts in sight when I climbed into another taxi.

4

In / Between

The police precinct looked like what I expected the stereo-typical TV show police station would. At first I was half expecting to see any one of the characters I'd grown up watching come out as I was heading for the door. Inside, however, was a different experience.

There was a large desk, stretching across two thirds of the room just a short way in from the door. A bored looking sergeant sat at one end clicking keys on a laptop behind a glass wall stretching the length of the bar. To his left, his colleague was dealing with the short line of people that had accumulated. There was a long bench off to my right where a ghost of a dark-haired woman was sat, picking dirt or something from her broken, chewed fingernails.

Beyond this large desk, a small collection of smaller desks were scattered about. Five desks in all. Each had a computer on them and some were occupied by a police officer. Not all the officers were alone, some were joined by people and ghosts. There was one empty desk.

I joined the line to see the desk sergeant behind two others already in line. There was a purple haired lady talking animatedly, and loudly, to the sergeant. She was trying to get her car that had been impounded.

'This is going to take a while I suspect,' said Henry.

I just nodded, I didn't want to draw attention to myself by speaking.

'Hey! You!' shouted someone from behind the main desk. This person, it was hard to describe them at first, was clearly a ghost. Their aura was blurring their form. Despite this lack of form, it was clear the ghost was looking right at me, or so I thought.

I looked about and no one else was reacting, apart from Henry and the woman sat on the bench. The aura of the woman on the bench changed from a light green and black combined, similar to the girl at the motel, to add in a little red.

The shouting person from behind the desk came charging towards me and they passed right through the desk and glass.

'I swore, Henry Costa, that I would kill you if I saw you ever again after what happened!' screamed the ghost.

Henry was backing away; his expression told me he didn't remember who this crazed apparition was. Raising my hands to call for a pause, I stepped in between Henry and the fast approaching banshee. I felt the force of the ghostly hands push against my heart and I flew back. Body remained standing there as I was flung through the wall and outside of the police building.

A moment later I saw Body running out of the building and down the street. Henry was reaching for my hand to help me up. 'What the hell was that?' I said.

'If we're quick-' Henry started to say.

I nodded and charged after Body. It was easy to move quickly in this form, I found. Henry was zipping along with me.

'Who is, or was, that?' I asked.

'I am loathe to contemplate, my friend. I do not believe that we met in life, and I know we've never met in the after either.'

Reaching Body and passing easily, I spun around to face myself. There was something behind my eyes, an unfamiliar expression coloured my face. The best description for what I saw was a mix of confusion and elation. Stop! I commanded Body.

For the briefest of moments, it appeared that Body wanted to comply, but then it kept on running. An unfamiliar voice spoke from my mouth.

'This is mine now, young man' Body gestured from my head down. A grin accompanied the sickly sweet tone.

'No!' I screamed. Anger burned as I lunged and grabbed the neck of Body with both hands.

My anger and the speed of my movement was enough to force out the occupying ghost. Body's forward movement was halted immediately as soon as I was back in Body, but now I was facing away from the thief who had forced me out.

Turning quickly on my heels, I could see the ghost being held down by Henry. 'We need a cleric. Someone that can do an exorcism,' said Henry through gritted teeth.

At the mention of an exorcism, the ghost immediately stopped thrashing.

'Please! No. I'll stop,' the ghost said. It's barely visible hands were raised in surrender.

'You're stopping yourself from moving on. Aren't you?' Henry said. He still held onto the ghost, his forearm was pressed up against its foggy throat.

I looked closer at the ghost, trying to see through the haze. It was impossible to see any details, its face was blurry, and the general outline of its body was unclear. It was like a cloud being blown gently apart at the edges.

'Why have you not moved over?' asked Henry. My friend was not letting go just yet.

'You! I hated what you did to my family and I swore I'd find you,' it replied.

'Your family? Who are you?' I said.

'My mother is, or was, Lady Amelia Larson-Bax. I'm her son, Samuel.'

At the mention of his name, Samuel's form started to solidify a little. I even thought I could see a pair of striking blue eyes twinkling through the haze.

'I remember her, it was my last case before falling ill. Lady Amelia lived in Edinburgh, huge house if I recall correctly. She was so upset at your sudden death, she wanted to prove you were still around, haunting her. To that end she hired a whole team of ghost hunters, myself included. There were even some from a fledgling television show I believe.

'I'd heard she moved to the US afterwards. I suspected it was to hide from the embarrassment. The TV show painted your mother in a very dim light. Made her appear, to all who saw, that she was, well, crazy.'

'She wasn't crazy!' Samuel screamed.

Henry started to relax his hold on Samuel. 'Why are you refusing to go into the light?' he asked with a softened tone as he spoke.

'You broke her heart!' Samuel said.

'I'm sorry you think that, but her heart was already broken when you died.' Henry looked sadder than I'd ever seen anyone. 'I never disputed her feelings, but we could not find evidence you were actually there. And that is what she so desperately wanted. Needed even. I am sorry your mother was caused more pain, that was never the intention.'

With awe and curiosity, I watched the conversation between the two ghosts. Henry was calmly and masterfully diffusing Samuel's anger. Samuel's form became more and more distinct as Henry continued.

'I bet she's waiting for you,' I said when the conversation took a natural pause.

They both turned to me like they'd forgotten I was there. Samuel smiled at the thought I'd planted and I saw his aura change through to an orange tint.

'Do you see that?' Samuel asked.

I shook my head as I recalled the light I saw in the operating room and Henry's response. 'We each see our own futures.'

There appeared to be a single tear on Samuel's cheek as he turned and then faded away.

'We should go back to the police,' said Henry.

'Has he-' I started to say.

'He moved on. It's what he should have done forty something years ago.' Henry paused a moment before finishing with, 'What will you say to the police for apparently running out?'

I could only shrug.

On the short walk back to the police precinct, I thought about how I was able to displace Samuel so easily, and without electricity of some form. I didn't have much time to consider the meaning before we were walking back through the doors of the police precinct. Worried about what they may think about Body having walked out before, I walked in as calmly as possible.

'Good afternoon, sir. How can I help?' said the desk sergeant. He didn't appear to recognise me, thankfully.

With a heavy sigh for effect, I first looked about the room, and then back to the sergeant. 'Is there someone I can talk to about the explosion at the conference centre? I believe my sister was working there the day it happened.'

Time seemed to slow down, two detectives were asking me question after question from then on. "Who was I?", "Where have I been?", "Why has it taken me so long to come forward?" and many similar ones.

It took a while, but eventually they finished and it felt like they believed me. The scars and stitches on my side showed I'd recently had surgery, and that definitely helped my explanation. They took my contact details and asked me to let them know when I was going to return home.

There was a point in their questioning me that they had a little double-take moment. One of the detectives had gone to review details of the staff on site at the explosion. Suze is basically my double, but in female form and with shoulder length hair. I've always had my hair close-cropped, and I've been a bit lazy with keeping in shape. The younger of the two detectives came back with a number of sheets he'd printed out with images of people believed to be working at the conference centre.

'That's Suze,' I said when the sheets were shown to me.

Eventually, after over an hour, the lead detective, a Lieutenant Gracie Roth, said she would let me know if anything comes up with the investigation.

When we left the precinct, Henry nodded to his right with an odd expression.

He pointed to his ear in frustration when I wasn't getting his clue. 'You want to pretend to be on a call to speak, remember.'

It took me a moment before I twigged. 'Oh, yes!' and I reached for my earbuds, putting the left one in my ear.

'Hey,' I said to the imaginary phone call.

'At last!' Henry said, exasperation in his tone. 'We're being followed, but don't look back.'

I didn't look. 'Living?' was all I replied with.

Henry gently shook his head. 'No.'

5

DIVIDE / OR OCCUPY

One thing I'd realised since my accident and seeing these ghosts was that they didn't have reflections. This meant that without turning around, I couldn't see our follower, and Henry was doing his best to ignore them but at the same time coyly trying to confirm we were still being followed.

There were too many people about for me to just stop and, for all to see, then start talking to thin air. The first few people who saw would possibly ignore me, but eventually someone would call for help. I needed to find a discreet place to confront our stalker ghost.

Between two buildings to my right there was an alley, I could see the industrial sized bins for a restaurant lining one wall. I decided this would be perfect to wait for our new friend, I ducked into the alley and waited.

Only a few seconds later, the ghost appeared around the corner of the building. It was a man dressed in what appeared to be a bloodstained business suit. There was a clear bullet wound in his upper chest. It startled him that we were standing there, waiting.

'Good afternoon,' I said.

He took a ghostly step back. 'I knew it! I knew you could see us. How are you doing that?' he asked.

'We are as perplexed as you,' said Henry.

The ghost jumped back again, he hadn't spotted Henry also waiting with me.

'Who are you?' I said.

'I'm Darryl Evans, I think. Yes, Darryl. Are you a Way Keeper? Or Keepers?' said Darryl, looking between myself and Henry. Then he turned to Henry, 'The ghost you helped to move on earlier, can you also help me?'

'How do you know he moved on?' Henry asked.

Darryl snorted. 'How else do you explain one of us just evaporating? I've been dead two years, I've seen others disappear while I've been taking to them. I've also seen two Christmases without my wife and children. They moved on, I'm stuck.'

'I am not sure it's as easy as that,' I replied.

Henry nodded. I could see that sadness in his eyes again. 'Without knowing more about you, I don't think we can help you,' he said.

Darryl's shoulders sagged and his head dropped. I felt really sorry we couldn't help him right there. 'That doesn't mean we're not going to be able to at some point,' I said.

Henry looked at me with surprise. Smiling, I hand waved his expression away.

'Listen, we can't help you right now. I'm trying to find my sister. But once I've made sure she's OK, we'll try to do what we can to help you,' I continued.

Darryl brightened and smiled between myself and Henry over and over. I reached out to shake Darryl by the hand. He was confused at first, but tentatively he reciprocated and we grasped each other's hands.

'I haven't spoken to anyone in nearly a year, and I've not touched a living, or any, person since-' his voice trailed off.

All I could do was smile.

'Well, looks like we will need more from you Darryl. Like your full name, date of birth, and obviously death. Maybe a few more details, and we could revisit your situation once we've resolved the current one.' Henry had turned all business, but I like how he immediately understood I really did want to help Darryl.

After the meeting with the police and the conversation with Darryl, I needed a few minutes to process. It had been a while since I'd eaten, that was on the plane. I stopped at a fast food place selling burgers and wings. Several minutes after speaking with Darryl, I'd been playing the conversation over and over. One thing kept coming back for attention as I ate.

'Henry, what is a Way Keeper?' I said.

Henry was sitting opposite to me and he was in his own thoughts. I coughed to catch his attention.

'A Way Keeper helps those stuck to finally cross over,' he said in a far away voice. He then turned to me, 'I think I know why you are here,' he said finally.

'I'm the Way Keeper?' I said, almost spitting out my burger in surprise.

'That would appear to be the case.'

In a daze over the possibility that my accident and the way my life has turned was not entirely random fate, I decided to take an Uber to as close to the explosion site as possible. The driver needed convincing, so I told him I was volunteering to help. I genuinely meant that too. If they wanted an extra pair of hands, I'd happily lend mine. Anything to distract me from the building anxiety that I'm somehow the saviour of ghost-kind was welcome at this point.

At the destroyed conference centre, surrounding a pile of rubble was a makeshift fence of police tape. There was a tent set up near what appeared to be the entrance, so I walked to there.

'Excuse me, sir, this area is restricted,' said a man in a yellow hi-vis jacket and hard hat.

'I'd like to help. Do you need any extra helpers?' I said.

He eyed me with a curious look.

'I think my sister was working here the day of the explosion. I need to do something.'

'But you're a Brit,' he stammered.

I nodded. 'Yes. And so is my sister, Suzanne Jones. She was working here, running the conference in fact.'

At the mention of my sister's name, the man's expression changed. 'We've not found her yet. We think Suze was in the main hall, which wasn't near to the explosion, but it was severely damaged when the building collapsed around it. The excavations haven't reached that area currently. We have to take it slow.'

'We're more than happy to have more help, though,' said a woman that joined us in the tent. 'Whatever you can do will be appreciated. I'm the site lead for this rescue, my name is Sara Thomas. And you are?'

Throughout the conversation, Henry had gone exploring and had now returned. 'I can see a few people in the rubble. Many are alive,' he said.

'I'm Jimmy Jones. Don't ask me how I know these things,' I said shaking Sara's hand, 'but I have a nose for finding things, or people, that can't be found.'

Sara smiled at me like I'd just told her I was actually insane. 'Jack, get Jimmy a jacket and hat. Let's put his nose to the test.'

'Henry, are there really any people still alive under all this crap?' I said when I was alone for a moment. 'I've been shovelling rocks for nearly two hours.'

I was covered in brick dust, my fingers and hands were all bruised and battered from digging in the rubble and my back was aching.

Henry nodded. 'I've been directing you to some, yes. There's a group of three over there,' he pointed to his right, about six feet ahead of me. I looked back the way I'd come and saw the path I'd cleared so far. 'One of them is seriously injured and may not last another hour. One of them is just unconscious, and the other is crying and praying but appears to be uninjured.'

'Thanks, I'll tell Jack.'

I saw Jack a few feet away talking to the guys holding a device they were using to scan the area. Another group had a couple of dogs with them. They'd been using the device and dogs to find people.

'Jack, mate, I think there are a few over there.' I pointed to where Henry had indicated.

The three men with the scanning device were all looking at me with scepticism.

I just waited. Jack shrugged and then nodded. 'Let's give this a go,' he said.

Moments later the guys with the scanner were all excitedly saying there were three people in the area I'd pointed out.

A burst of activity followed.

The first person found was the seriously injured person. A woman in her forties, I guessed. She was impaled on a steel rod going through her abdomen. The next was the praying one. He was a young man, in his early twenties probably, and he was so grateful. He kept telling the rescue squad that God would look after him. The third was an unconscious man. He was probably in his fifties, maybe older. The prognosis was not good from what I'd overheard the medic assessing him say.

Getting the survivors I'd found free from the rubble was slow going. It was dark by the time we freed them all.

It had been a very long day. I couldn't recall when I last slept, my body was running on pure adrenaline at this point. I was sat on the kerb with a cold bottle of water in my hand when Sara joined me. She gave me a warm burrito wrapped in paper and foil.

'You're our good luck charm, Jimmy,' she said. 'You deserve that, and more.'

'Told you,' I chuckled while tapping my nose.

She laughed with me. 'You're coming back tomorrow, right?'

I'd not seen many ghosts at the site, which was surprising, but in some ways it was understandable. The most I'd seen were staying outside the perimeter tape. I assumed the ghosts of any of the dead under the rubble were probably either already passed on, or they had gone seeking some help like Darryl did.

'I hope to be. I'm just looking for Suze, I haven't heard from her since the explosion. It's not looking good. My heart wants to believe she's not under all this.' I waved at the broken building behind me.

She hugged me with one arm and got up to leave, 'I hope she's not there too.'

Before I could reply, I saw someone across the street. Her long brown hair was tied into a pony tail, and she was wearing a dark baseball hat, but even through the darkness of the evening, I could tell it was Suze.

I was about to call out to her when I noticed the aura around her.

'Well, I'm going to go home to take a shower. Maybe I'll see you tomorrow,' Sara said as she was packing away her things.

'Maybe,' I replied with a smile. I tried to keep one eye on my sister while saying bye to Sara.

When Sara was out of earshot, I looked for Henry. He was standing at my side and had already spotted Suze. 'Henry, she's over there. Don't make it obvious, but take a look at that person over there with the purple and green aura. That's Suze! Or at least, that's her body. Someone else is home, though, I think,' I hissed.

6

— • —

SUZE / BUT NOT

'I'm shattered, I really need sleep, but I can't let her go now!' I said to Henry.

'Go home. Get some rest. I'll keep an eye on her, and whoever is occupying her.' Henry patted my shoulder. The fact I was not doing this alone was a massive comfort.

My day seemed to be filled with taking Ubers and taxis. Leaving Henry to follow Suze, I waited for another to come and collect me. As I was leaving, I watched the rescue crews do a shift change. People would be working through the night and News crews were still around recording the events. This was a 24 hour operation.

At Suze's apartment I took a shower and then headed to the guest room. The door intercom buzzed as I was about to close the bedroom door and I was tempted to not answer it; my tired brain was not ready for dealing with any more.

In the end the buzzing was insistent, so I pressed the talk button on the intercom to reply. 'Hello?' I was surprised to see it didn't have a screen.

'I'm looking for someone,' replied an unfamiliar male voice.

'Hey, happy to help, but you buzzed me. Who is this?' I said.

'Where's Suzanne Jones?'

'OK,' I was tired and done with pleasantries, 'I think you need to tell me who you are now.'

There was no answer, and after a moment of waiting I released the talk button. I shook off a shiver down my spine. After checking the apartment door was locked, it was time for sleep.

My sleep was full of disturbing images of people trapped under brick rubble, broken concrete slabs and other debris.

The impaled woman was smiling at me asking me to help her. She kept pointing to the unconscious man we found. The words she said were a jumble, so I had to rewind the dream a few times. I wanted to replay the words she said. On the final attempt, it sounded like she was trying to say, "He did it".

With those words ringing in my brain, my eyes shot open.

I was surprised to see the morning light outside. I'd forgotten to pull down the blind over the window, but it was good to feel the sun warming me through the glass. It looked like another warm Orlando day ahead.

When I emerged from the bedroom, Henry was waiting for me in the living room.

'Good morning.' Henry didn't wait for me to properly wake up. 'I followed her around the city, keeping a safe distance, of course. I do not know if the ghost within her would be able to spot another spirit following,' he finished. I could tell by his expression he was hiding something.

'Go on,' I urged.

'She tried this building, and I am certain she buzzed this apartment because the person who answered sounded like you.'

It dawned on me that my late-night visitor was Suze, or whoever was driving her body. Another thought occurred; does that mean Suze is still alive but trapped in ghost form? How else would her body have known to come here, or her name?

'But she didn't stay?' I said when the whirlwind of thoughts calmed down.

Henry shook his head. 'I followed her to a homeless shanty town outside the city centre. I left a fellow spirit called Amos to watch her while I came here and gave you an update.'

'Do you think she is still there?'

'Hard to say. The physical body at least appeared to be tired, she clearly needed sleep. I don't know much about the ghost inhabitant.'

'Thanks', I said. 'I'll get dressed and we can head down there.'

The homeless shanty town occupied a derelict area of land surrounded on three sides by a broken chain-link fence. It was filled with dusty, grimy tents, torn tarpaulins, cardboard and piles of rubbish. An old man with no teeth, sitting in an old wheelchair, was dozing near one of the old tents. As I approached, I noticed his left leg had been amputated near to the hip.

'Spare a buck?' he sputtered through his gums when he saw me getting near.

I offered a five dollar bill to him and he acted like it was Christmas. 'I'm looking for my sister. She looks like me. We're twins,' I said to the old man.

'She may be sleeping. Last I saw of her anyways. Over there,' he pointed to a black tarp near the back of this area of land.

Henry sped off ahead, moving easily through the solid obstacles. I had to slowly pick my way over broken glass, rubbish strewn here and there, and through a maze of overturned shopping carts and makeshift tents.

Before I could get all the way across, Henry was already returning. 'She's gone, and so has Amos, the spirit I'd asked for help.'

On our way out back to the street, the old man piped up, 'Did yer find his sister?' He was looking only at Henry. Henry turned, startled.

Stopping in my tracks, I spotted the $5 bill on the floor beneath the old man's chair and realised he was a ghost. The fact that the money had fallen straight through the old man's hands when I'd given it hadn't registered to me at all. Also, I now realised his aura was white, like the tarpaulin behind him, which was probably why I didn't spot it at first.

I wanted to ask him how long he'd been dead, but I didn't want to sound rude. My silence didn't matter, the old man saw my question. 'More than forty years this summer, I reckon,' he said.

'And you don't want to cross over?' Henry asked.

'Never seen a need to. Happy enough here,' the old man said. 'Don't believe I ever seen a Way Keeper before though,' he said as he finished and turned, pointedly, to me.

'Why don't you want to go to the after?' I asked, remembering what Henry had called the point of existence after death.

'Don't believe in it,' he said. 'Besides, I like seeing the world and meeting new people all the time.'

'Do you know Amos? Do you know where he went?' Henry said.

The old man thought for a moment, looked over at the black tarp I'd tried to get to, and then back to us. 'Amos went to some contention place, I believe.'

'The conference centre?' Henry and I both said at the same time.

'That makes more sense. Yeah, a conference place. He wants a conference. Happy trails, I'm going to my sister's old place. I see you have a defender already, but if you ever need advice,' he turned and looked directly at me, 'you come looking for me. You'll find me here most days.'

With those as his final words, he was already floating away, ghostly wheelchair and all. His voice was trailing off as he went.

'We need to be at the centre again anyway,' I said to Henry.

Henry looked at me with a smirk.

'Not for her. For Suze,' I said. I felt my face flush at the thought of Sara.

'Of course,' Henry said still smiling.

'We've not had much chance to talk about this situation,' I said as we arrived back at the conference centre. 'But I need to know more about Way Keepers, and why I appear to be one.'

Henry didn't breathe, he didn't need to, but I was sure I heard him take a deep breath and slowly release it. 'A Way Keeper is rare. When I was alive I heard of them and I did some research, obviously. As part of the job. I met a few who claimed they were Way Keepers, but I never met anyone who was genuine. In my line of work, you meet many a scam artist.'

'How rare is rare?' I asked.

'In my research, the details differed. Somewhere between every hundred years or every thousand. However, even then, nothing was documented about how they are created, how they know or how they come to learn how to do what they do. If, indeed, they do exist you appear to be living proof.'

Before I could reply, I saw that Sara had spotted me and was already walking over.

'I think the fact you can split yourself, and others can inhabit your Body means you are the key to helping those that are stuck. Samuel was able to cross over after inhabiting you, so that seems to fit the theory,' Henry finished. He then drifted off into the rubble. I assumed he was looking for survivors.

'Hey, you're back!' Sara said as she reached me. 'Ready to put your nose to work again?' She tapped her nose and giggled a little as she spoke.

7

Capture / Release

Whilst helping out again at the conference centre, I was keeping a weather eye out for Suze, hoping to see her, hoping to be able to talk to her.

In our searching and sifting, Henry and I, with the help of the other rescue crews, found a few more survivors. We were so successful that the guys using the scanning equipment and dogs often came to us, to me specifically, to confirm their findings. Each time, I pretended to look in the directions given and concentrate while Henry scouted out the area.

During lunch I excused myself, saying I had a call. I felt the need to talk to Henry.

'Henry, I.don't have many people in my life. I was between jobs before my accident, Suze had moved away, and our parents are both dead. I know we haven't known each other that long, but I hope you know that I trust our friendship. And right now, it's really nice to have a friend,' I said.

'I value your company too,' Henry replied.

'I hope you don't think I'm trying to take advantage of the fact you can do things us mere mortals can't.'

'Oh, I know you are.' Henry smiled as he spoke; a friendly, happy smile. I could see he was playing with me. 'Do not be concerned, though, I am fully on your side here. I want to help any and all of the poor, unfortunate souls trapped here if I can. If that means pretending you are able to sense people who are trapped, then I cannot see any problem with that.'

'Thank you,' I smiled back.

We spent another two hours hunting for more trapped people. Henry was able to point out a few of the dead, and I could see his heart sink further every time he did. The only consolation was their spirits appeared to have already crossed over to the after.

In the middle of the afternoon, I saw Lieutenant Roth and her partner had arrived at the conference centre. They were talking to Sara, who then pointed in my direction.

'Doesn't look good, James,' Henry said in my ear.

I shook my head in agreement. 'Hello?' I said once they reached me.

'Mr. Jones, could you come down to the station? We have something for you to look at, and it would help us too if you could answer a few more questions.'

She sounded all serious and professional; not at all like when I'd last spoken to her. Before she sounded caring and concerned.

'What's happened?' I asked.

'It's best if you could come with us.

'How did you know I was here?' I asked before spotting a woman I'd seen a few times before, but not really registered her presence, talking to two police officers in uniform that had also arrived. 'You had me followed? Am I being arrested for something?'

'Please, Mr. Jones,' Roth said, hand on her hip where her cuffs were attached.

Seeing no other choice at this point, I sighed and gestured for her to lead the way. She merely stepped aside and allowed me to pass by.

As I got nearer to the uniformed officers, they started to approach, but in the corner of my eye I saw Roth raise a hand to tell them to step back.

My fight or flight reaction was screaming at me to run, but I knew I'd done nothing wrong. For now, I would play along.

At the police precinct, I was taken to a room labelled Interview 2. In the room, I was almost pushed into the chair by Roth's partner. The last time I was here, I spoke to Roth in her office.

'What's going on here? Do I need a lawyer, or something? I've lost my sister, I'm trying to help out at the conference centre and you are treating me like a criminal. Is this how you treat people worried about their lost or missing family?' I was staring deadeye at Roth's partner.

Keeping my voice even, all politeness had left my tone.

Henry nudged me. 'Careful, don't poke the beast.'

'We want to show you a video,' Roth said and she spun her laptop around so I could see the screen. 'Please, press the space bar.'

Henry had moved from my side and was now standing behind the detectives. He had a clear view of the notes and files the detectives had with them. I paused a moment and looked at Henry quickly before I returned my gaze to the laptop screen. Roth and her partner were too busy looking at the laptop to notice my hesitation.

Confused, I tentatively pressed the space bar to start the video. The black and white footage was of the entrance hall of the precinct, where we'd first met the spirit of Samuel Larson-Bax.

If I didn't look nervous before, I did now. I saw myself jerk back and then head out of the precinct at quite a pace.

'I get nervous with crowds,' I said. It was the first thing I could think of to say.

'Crowds?' said Roth's partner. He still hadn't introduced himself. 'There's hardly anyone there.'

'This isn't all, is it Mr. Jones?' Roth chimed in before she reached over and paused the video.

I gave her my best blank look as she placed two photos before me. They were zoomed in stills of me at the time Samuel forced me out of Body.

The first photo was of my whole body, in an awkward pose where my back was arched and my face contorted into a painful grimace. The second was an image of my face and chest area. My expression was transformed into a lifeless stare.

The worry, for me at least, was the apparent burst of something cloud-like around my chest on both images.

'We can be photographed?' Henry shouted. Alarm was clear in his voice.

Only I heard him, and I tried hard not to look at or speak to him directly.

'What is this, Mr. Jones?' Roth asked as she tapped the second image, her chewed fingernail pointing straight to the wispy collection around my chest.

I thought about being flippant. I honestly wanted to tell them to get a new camera. However, I thought my responses would not be taken with the level of sarcasm I wanted to convey. Instead, I opted for blissful honesty. 'Looks like a digital image artefact,' I said.

Well, honesty with a touch of subterfuge.

'You then returned around twenty minutes later,' said Partner-cop.

'OK. Is that an issue? Did I do something wrong?'

Partner-cop then pressed the space bar to start playback of another video. I watched myself enter, walk over to and then talk to the desk sergeant. They let the video continue until it ended. I shrugged.

'Can't see anything there. That white cloud thing is not there either,' I said.

'You visited an area downtown this morning. We have eye-witness reports of you talking to yourself.' Roth said.

Images of the old man in a wheelchair came back to me, alongside a memory of the woman I had seen at the conference centre. 'Was that this morning?'

At the mention of me talking to myself, I had a bright idea. I reached into my trouser pocket and pulled out my earbuds case, held it up and shrugged and then replaced them in my pocket.

'Again, I ask you, what have I done wrong with any of this? Is it a crime to not like crowded places? Is it a crime to allegedly talk to oneself? All of these things you are talking about are more than a little reaching to be honest. Any lawyer would throw this all out and you know it,' I said.

I wouldn't let either of them interrupt me while I spoke and I saw Partner-cop getting angrier and angrier with each syllable I uttered. Roth was clearly looking uncomfortable in my questioning back.

'We ask the questions here!' Partner-cop shouted while rising out of his chair.

'Edmonds!' Roth said, placing a hand on the shoulder of Partner-cop.

There was a knock at the door and it was quickly opened. A tall woman in a grey and white business suit and high heels walked in. 'Roth, my office. Now. Both of you.'

Henry had followed the trio and returned a few minutes later. 'The captain, lovely lady, has torn a strip or two off them both. They are heading this way to release you.'

A second later, the door opened and Edmonds came in to the room. He leant against the mirror, his face was a picture of angry embarrassment. He looked at the floor rather than at me and said, 'You can leave.' He then gestured to the open door.

I didn't speak, I just stood and walked out. In the corridor the captain spoke. 'Mr. Jones, I'd like to apologise. Can we talk?'

Keeping my silence, I nodded and waited for the captain to begin. She led me to her office as she started to talk.

'I understand your hesitation with unfamiliar situations,' her eyes were telling me that she really didn't understand. 'My detectives can be a little demanding at times. We believe there may be a criminal element to the explosion. The Fire Department Office of Fire Investigations are still conducting investigations. We can't rule anything out at this stage.'

'Someone did this on purpose?' I asked.

'We don't have enough information to say at this point. My detectives are quite keen to resolve this as soon as possible, so I understand the emotions.'

'Edmonds had family in the conference centre, didn't he?' I read between the lines when I saw her face.

The captain's silence confirmed my suspicions. She quickly changed subject. 'I want to assure you that we are doing all that we can to find your sister.'

'Thank you,' I said.

'Please take my card. If you need anything, do not hesitate to call me.' The captain then handed me her business card.

I pocketed the card and said my goodbye.

Henry was waiting in reception. He was talking to a ghost, and I heard them mentioned Suze as I approached. 'James, this is Amos.'

Amos nodded to me. 'A pleasure to meet you, Way Keeper.'

I tried to hide the embarrassment of the title he gave me.

'Amos says that he unfortunately lost your sister, Suzanne,' said Henry.

'I am sorry,' said Amos.

I shook my head to say it wasn't a problem. Heading for the exit, I tried to make sure I was not overheard speaking to anyone before I was outside.

On the street I stopped walking and the two ghosts looked at me with curious eyes.

'I have a plan,' I said.

8

THEORIES / WAY KEEPER

I signalled a taxi from those parked nearby that I wanted to take a ride and waited for the driver to pull over to our side of the street.

'Amos, can you go everywhere you can, and gather some of our friends. Ask them to meet me at the conference centre. I am going to need help. Lots of it,' I said to Amos.

He nodded. 'I will be there.'

The taxi arrived before me and once inside the car I directed the driver to take me to my sister's building. Henry nudged me as we drove. It took me a moment to realise it was the same taxi I had taken the day I arrived.

By habit from my multiple taxis over the last couple of days, I'd taken a seat in the back and hadn't registered the familiar female ghost sat in the passenger seat. When I turned to look forward, she was staring at me.

'You are special, yes?' she said in a heavy Jamaican twang.

Henry answered for me. 'That has been said, yes.'

She looked at Henry sternly, he raised his hands in mock surrender.

'Hey,' I said to the driver, 'Do you enjoy driving people around the city?'

'Yeah, it's the best job. It's never the same day to day, you meet all sorts of interesting people.' The driver was as amiable as the last time we met.

'What do your parent's think of your profession?'

'My mom died a few years back,' he paused as he made a right turn. I appreciated him concentrating on the driving. 'Never met my dad. Mom always wanted me to be happy, and I wish I could tell her that I am.'

The ghost in the passenger seat turned to her son and beamed with pride. 'Can you tell him that I am?' she looked directly at me.

'You know, I believe if you are happy and enjoying what you do then I can't see how she would fail to see that also. From wherever she may be now.' I smiled at the driver through the rear-view mirror.

Our eyes locked, and he smiled back. 'Yeah, I am sure she's smiling down on me right now.'

'You have no idea,' mumbled Henry.

'Thank you,' said the driver's mother. She placed a loving hand on his shoulder and then slowly began to cross over to the after as we drove. Her smile was the last part of her to go.

The driver caught his breath when, with a silent pop, her smile disappeared. I saw a tear slowly roll from his eye and I reached over to give his shoulder a gentle squeeze. He replied with a happy smile.

'Well, my theory has been tested, and proven false,' Henry said as we rode the elevator in my sister's apartment building.

'Theory?' I said.

'The theory a ghost has to enter your body to be able to pass over. The taxi driver's mother passed to the after with a short conversation. However, that sparks a new theory. An amendment of the original, if you will, one closely linked to my first one.'

I looked at Henry, waiting for him to continue.

'Your presence, your ability to see the ghosts and talk to them, is all that is needed. The ghosts wish to be seen, and you are seeing them. Being seen is helping them to cross into the next stage of their,' Henry paused, looking for the right word, 'existence.'

'You nearly said "life" there didn't you?' I said with a smirk.

Henry stayed silent, and then he laughed. I joined in until the elevator doors opened. The flush of embarrassment I felt rushed through my face as an old woman stepped past me and into the elevator as I was stepping out.

We entered Suze's apartment, and I began laughing again.

'What's funny now?' Henry asked.

'My life. I never once expected this turn of events. In fact, I never expected a life at all a few weeks ago. Now I am alive, I can separate my physical and spiritual, ghostly, selves. No idea how that works. I also appear to be some sort of nexus for helping the dead to gain peace.'

Henry watched me as I went to the bedroom. I could tell he wanted to say something, but all I could think about right now was Suze and finding her.

'Why are we here?' Henry asked.

I was fishing in my bag as he spoke. My hand rested on something hard and slightly sharp at the bottom, and I grabbed it and pulled gently. 'This!' I said.

I held up a necklace. It was a little silver boy on a chain. 'It's half of a shared thing and Suze has the other half, a girl shaped piece, that interlocks with mine. Our Grandma gave them to us when we were born. The first twins in the family. It's silver, see,' and I showed the mark to Henry.

He tried to squint at it, but then leant back and looked at me. 'How will this trinket help our cause?'

'When we were kids,' I chuckled at the thoughts and memories that were flooding through my brain, 'we told everyone these were magical. That with this, no one could separate us.'

I held the little silver boy to the light of the window. 'I'm going to use this as a form of a compass. I'm hoping this is going to pull Suze to me.'

'Items revered with the love of a child, or two, are the most powerful,' Henry said.

'Careful.' I turned away from the window to look at Henry, 'You're starting to sound like one of those nuts you used to debunk.'

Henry smiled at my obvious joke. 'Don't misunderstand me. In life I was a sceptic to rival all sceptics, but my death and my continued existence has given me an evolving perspective.' He emphasised the word "existence" with slow deliberation.

'Now, after we get some cash at the ATM down the road, to pay for yet more taxis, we need to head to the conference centre again.'

'Would it not be more prudent to hire a vehicle?' Henry asked.

'I don't have a driving licence?'

Henry looked at me curiously and I shook my head.

'I failed my test. Twice. I haven't plucked up the courage to try again,' I said.

Across the street from the destroyed conference centre, I saw the old man in the wheelchair again. Next to him was Amos, and three other ghosts. Including Darryl.

'Hello Darryl, are you here to help me?'

'Of course I am, I will do anything I can to help you,' Darryl said.

'I am Aretha,' said one of the other ghosts.

'You are the Way Keeper?' scoffed the remaining ghost. Its tone dripped with distaste.

I could only smile at this group.

'These are all I could gather, Way Keeper,' said Amos.

'You did well. Thank you,' I said to Amos. He appeared thankful.

I looked around to ensure no one living could see or hear me. We were across the street from the conference centre, the exact spot I last saw Suze standing on. 'I'm looking for my sister. She should be easy to recognise, because she looks like me, but with longer hair. We're twins.'

Darryl shifted uncomfortably. 'How can we help? She's living. Only someone like you, a Way Keeper, can see or hear us.'

'True,' I agreed, 'but she's not home. At least that is what appears to be the case. Some other ghost is inside her body. I think if her spirit is not inside her own body, then it must be in there.' I pointed at the conference centre.

'And you need us to look in the rubble?' Amos asked.

'Exactly.' Henry said for me. 'I have been through parts of the centre, but it is too large for me alone. James has had a great idea here, and more of us should be able to cover more of the site.'

With that said, Amos and the others headed for the conference centre. Henry waited a moment.

'She may have passed over to the after on her own,' Henry said when the others were far enough away.

'I know, but I have a theory of my own,' I replied.

Henry nodded and began to follow the others.

'Thank you, my friends,' I said to their retreating backs. 'Henry, I will try to find Sara to get an update. I'll meet you all over in that diner,' I pointed across the street, 'in an hour.'

Henry bowed his head slightly in acknowledgement as he continued off into the rubble.

Taking a deep breath, I crossed the street. Jack, the site foreman, was the first to see me approaching.

'Jimmy, I didn't expect to see you again today,' he said.

'Well, I couldn't leave you in the lurch. Is Sara about?'

'She left about an hour ago. Probably won't be back until tomorrow. She looked tired, man.'

Behind him, there was not much movement and there was only one news crew remaining. Yesterday there were five crews.

'What's going on?' I asked.

'We're shutting down tomorrow.' Jack looked crestfallen. 'We haven't been able to find anything or anyone most of the day. Since you left, in fact. Also, from our records, we probably found everyone we can. Dead or alive. Barring a miracle, if there are any more people in there it has been too long now to find anyone remaining alive. The search and rescue guys have stood down agreeing with that assessment.'

I was confused.

'I know,' he continued. 'That means your sister-'

'She's alive. I've seen her,' I said. The relief that crossed over Jack's face was quickly replaced with confusion. 'She was over there last night before I left, but I lost her. I think she may be injured, a bang to the head maybe. I don't know. But something drew her back here at least once.'

Jack could only nod.

'How long has that news crew been here?' I asked.

'They have been here from the start.'

'Care to introduce me?' I asked.

Jack shrugged. 'I want to see where this goes.'

9

NEWS / NO NEWS

There was only one news crew remaining, a yellow and blue van bearing the name "News Pulse 7". I saw three people packing away equipment around the van.

'Hello,' I said to a short man who'd stopped working as we approached. 'I'm Jimmy Jones.' I offered a handshake.

'You're the "Brit with a Heart", yeah, I've seen you about. I'm Nolan Webber, we're News Pulse 7.' While shaking my hand, Webber gestured to the other two; a bald woman with a deep suntan and a gangly, greasy haired young lad who's pale skin told me he never goes out in the sun. 'That's Greta, and this is my nephew Harris.'

I nodded to each of them. Greta carried on working without missing a beat; she was tying up cables in neat coils. Harris was carrying two large cans that I assumed contained generator fuel.

'This is Jack,' I paused as I realised I'd never learned his full name. 'Sorry, Jack, I never asked.'

Jack smiled and offered his own handshake. 'Jack Waller.'

Webber shook Jack's hand too.

'I'm looking for my sister, my twin.' I looked Webber directly in the eyes trying not to be intimidating. I wanted this man to offer his help. 'Do you have any crowd shots? I saw her here myself, but she didn't see me. We, I tried to follow her, but I lost her. I'm worried she's injured and doesn't realise it.'

'We're a small, independent crew. We put most of our footage up on YouTube. Why would she be here?' Webber asked.

'She was the site organiser for the tech expo scheduled here,' Jack said.

'We wondered what your interest in this was,' piped up Greta, in a strong New York accent. She still hadn't stopped working and was now dismantling an awning attached to the side of the van.

'Our channel is called "News Pulse 7", like the van,' Harris added.

'Mr. Webber,' I started to say.

'Nolan, please,' interrupted Webber.

'Nolan,' I said, 'could I ask if you would keep your eyes peeled when editing your videos. If you see my sister, you can't miss her, she looks exactly like me, can you get in touch? I'll give you my email address.'

'It would be a pleasure. For a price, of course,' Webber said. A teasing smile crossed his face. 'If you agree to an interview,' he finished.

'Absolutely,' I said. 'Something that may help identify her is the other half of this. She has a girl that hugs this boy when they connect,' I held up my half of the necklace; it spun gently.

'She'll likely be wearing her half, because it's not in her apartment where I've been staying,' I finished.

After Webber and his crew and I had swapped contact details, and he'd taken a photo of my necklace, we said our goodbyes. It was getting late and I'd not eaten. While Jack stayed to talk to Greta, I headed to the diner to wait for Henry.

I was the only customer at the diner, Marie, my waitress had already given me three cups of coffee whilst I waited. A half-eaten meal before me had gone cold.

'Not hungry, sir,' said Marie, coffee pot in hand.

Rousing myself from my ruminations, I looked up at her smiling face. 'Sorry. Can't eat. The food's lovely, but I have a lot on my mind.'

'Don't tell me, it's all about a girl.'

'In a way, yes. My sister. She worked over there.' I pointed to the rubble of the conference centre.

'That must be hard for you. They haven't found her?'

'No, but I think she may have got out. We haven't found a body, I just don't know where she is. I hope they are right and she escaped. Unfortunately, the rescue crew are stopping the search; it's been too long to find anyone alive now. It's just a case of finding if there are any bodies remaining in there.'

'I can see why you're worried,' Marie said.

Through the diner windows, I saw Henry approaching.

'How much do I owe you?' I asked as I started to stand.

Marie shook her head. 'It's on the house. I hope you find your sister.'

'Thank you,' I said.

Outside the diner, Henry was alone.

'The others are continuing to search. There are no spirits in the wreckage, I'm certain. However, I saw one body, vindicating the rescue crew's decision to stop.' Henry's face was full of concern.

'Thank you. I wasn't expecting a great deal, to be honest.' I paused as a memory of her surfaced. 'When we saw her standing here, there was something off about her aura,' I said.

'Off?'

'It looked like there was more than one soul fighting for dominance. I've seen ghosts more than I ever really wanted to, and one thing I know about is the aura each of them have. They usually only have one colour.' I paused to search for the right way to explain what I saw.

'Suzanne had two colours,' said Henry.

'Exactly! There was a dark green, almost black colour and a bright yellow. The two shifted about her. If Suze is anywhere, I bet she's still in her own body. Somehow the spirit that caused this is there also.'

'How do we proceed?'

'I need to speak to Sara, or Jack.'

I looked over to where the News Pulse 7 van had been parked and saw they had left. Jack was no-where to be seen either. The night security guard was sitting in the entry way of the derelict building, under the awning of a tent that had been placed there as a shelter doubling as an office space.

Dozing in his chair, he tried to pretend he hadn't been asleep when I approached.

'We're not doing any rescues tonight, Jimmy,' he said.

'I know, Theo, I just have a question and you may know the answer,' I said.

Theo looked at me with a question of his own.

'The survivors we pulled out, do you know which hospital they may have been taken to?'

Henry twigged immediately. 'The man from your dream?'

'Yeah, sure. They would probably have been taken to Regional, ORMC,' Theo said.

'Many thanks. See you later.' I walked away from the tent. 'We'll have to go tomorrow. Visiting hours will be well and truly over for the day,'

Breakfast was more like lunch, I'd slept in late. At around 11am, I'd ordered an Uber to take me to ORMC and I was now standing in the entry concourse. 'Henry, can you see if you can find our friend?'

Henry nodded and sped off.

A member of staff approached me while I stood there looking lost. 'Can I help you, sir?' she said. Her white coat told me she was a doctor.

'Hopefully. I've been volunteering at the conference centre rescue because I've been trying to find my sister,' I said.

'What is her name?' said the doctor.

'Suze. Suzanne Jones. I don't think she is here, but I'm just trying to do what I can. She has long dark hair, and looks a little like myself, obviously.' I didn't want to mention being twins, I felt like I'd harped on about that aspect a little too much lately.

'Of course.' She lifted her tablet and typed in a few details. 'I'm not seeing her name, but we have three unknown women in ICU. If you are feeling up to it, can you look at a couple of images? See if one of them is your sister?'

I nodded my agreement, and she pulled up three photos side-by-side on screen. One of the images was a black woman, her hair was plastered to her forehead with sweat. Another was of an elderly white woman with long white hair. Both of these I dismissed immediately.

The third woman had long dark hair, and the breathing mask she wore obscured her face a little too much. 'Can you zoom in on her a little?' I said.

'I can take you there and you can have a closer look,' she said.

'Lead the way.'

A minute or two later, we were looking through a window into ICU where the woman with the dark hair was visible. The real-life view, rather than a still photo, was much clearer.

'She has a tattoo in the crook of her arm, here on her left,' I said, pointing to my own arm. 'Our aunt went mad when she came home with it. It's our parents initials either side of a broken heart with a halo.'

'Let me check,' she said. 'Wait here please.'

I watched as she went into the ICU, grab some blue latex gloves and then reach for the woman's left arm. A moment later, she was returning. 'There's no tattoo, I'm sorry.'

'Thank you for checking, I'll try another hospital.'

On my way out, Henry found me. 'I found him. He is awake, but unresponsive. If I were a doctor, I would say he was cata- tonic.'

'Follows the theory then,' I said.

As I continued towards the door, I saw a ghost, a teenaged girl around 19 years old, approach me. Our eyes had connected and I saw her face brighten when she saw that I had seen her.

'Can you see me?' asked the ghost. 'They keep saying I died to my parent's, but I am right here. I haven't died. Can you tell them, please?'

Her pleading broke my heart. Tears were flowing down her translucent face as she pointed to a collection of seats to my right.

'Unfortunately, Miss, I am afraid the doctors are correct,' said Henry.

I looked over to the waiting area the teenager pointed out and I saw a couple sitting there, arm in arm, crying.

'What is your name?' I asked.

'Bethany Morgan. My parents are Andrew and Joan,' Bethany replied.

I walked over to the Morgans. 'Can I sit with you?'

Andrew Morgan nodded, his wife had her head down and her eyes were closed. Tears were streaking her make up on her face.

'Mr. Morgan, I know this must be hard, but if you want to talk to someone, I can offer a sympathetic ear,' I said.

'Who are you? Do you work here?' Joan said as she looked up at me.

'I don't work here. I am here on vacation to see my sister, but she was involved in the explosion recently. I haven't been able to find her, despite searching the rubble,' I said.

'Are you a grief counsellor? Who are you?' Morgan asked. His tone was stern and suspicious.

I shook my head. 'My name is Jimmy Jones. I am not a counsellor, but I can see you are hurting more than most here right now and it broke my heart to see your pain. I wanted to offer any help I could.'

'Unless you can bring back my daughter, there is nothing you can do,' said Morgan. He then turned away from me to indicate the conversation was over.

Joan was still looking at me with hope.

'Take my number. When you are ready, I will be there.' I then gave Joan a slip of paper I'd written my name and number on, and then I left them to their grief.

Returning to Bethany, I could see she had too many questions. 'Stay close to them. They won't be able to see or hear you, but they may get some comfort from your presence. And so will you. When they are ready, they might call me, and then I can help you all.'

'Thank you for trying.'

10

—·—

Searching / Finding

Henry and I left the hospital and rather than immediately taking yet another Uber I opted to walk for a spell. The evening air was still warm, the almost daily Floridian rain a couple of hours earlier today had taken the temperature down to a bearable level, and the light breeze was more than welcome.

I didn't speak as I walked, I just allowed my thoughts to drift; trying, for a brief moment, to forget the chaos of the last few days. Henry was content to travel alongside me, also keeping his silence.

Following nothing but my feet one in front of the other, I found I'd headed towards a pizzeria. My grumbling stomach was all the convincing I needed to head across the road and enter.

Inside it was just as I expected, and the food smelled amazing.

A server, a lad probably just out of his teens approached me. 'Table for one, sir?'

'That'll be fantastic,' I replied.

He led me over to a table by the window facing the busy road. Two police cars and an ambulance came screaming past as I watched the traffic.

'This is not the best of neighbourhoods,' said Henry. It was the first time he'd spoken in nearly thirty minutes and I almost jumped out of my skin.

'Are you ok, sir?' the server asked me as he handed me a menu. Concern crossed his face when I jumped.

'Everything is fine. Can I have a pepperoni pizza?' I spluttered.

'One pepperoni coming right up. Do you want anything to drink?' The lad still held onto the menu I'd not taken from his hand.

'Beer?'

While in the pizzeria I'd ordered another Uber to collect me. I didn't fancy the long walk to Suze's apartment.

A woman in a 1950s style diner outfit had been flitting about the restaurant. Passing through the walls clearly marked her out as a ghost, she kept looking over at me and Henry. I tried to keep any chatter between us quiet; I didn't want people to think I was actually talking to myself. However, Diner-Lady noticed Henry and would howl at us whenever she spotted us talking.

Diner-Lady hadn't approached me while I ate, which I was really thankful for, and I was glad to get into the Uber when it arrived.

The journey back to Suze's apartment was quiet, my driver didn't speak beyond introducing herself and confirming my name when she collected me. It was nice to have a break to myself; it gave me a chance to take stock.

At first, I just reviewed the car, how clean it was and how it smelled so inviting. The driver herself was smartly dressed and her perfume was not overpowering. A tattoo could be seen creeping from under the cuff of her right sleeve.

On the street, people were carrying on with their lives and were oblivious to the ghosts that I could see wandering the streets too.

A truck was taking a right up ahead, through the red light. The "right on red" thing is something I will never get used to seeing. Crossing the road before the truck was a woman holding the hand of a child. Initially, I was about to call out, warn the woman, or the driver, but then I saw their aura and realised they were ghosts.

It then struck me that there had been more than one occasion where I have not immediately noticed I was seeing ghosts; just like the old-timer in the wheelchair. It shocked me a little that I could not always immediately tell when someone was not alive.

'We're here,' said the driver as she pulled up and stopped the car.

I hadn't realised we had stopped until she spoke.

'Sorry, was in my own little world then. Thank you,' I said as I exited the car.

On the street I took in a deep breath as I stretched up to my full height. The night air was refreshing, despite the fumes from the passing traffic.

'James. Isn't that your sister?' Henry brought me out of my reverie.

I looked at him and then across the street to where he pointed. My sister was stood there, staring at the building.

'Suze!' I called out, and she looked straight at me.

Our eyes locked, but I could see that Suze was not recognising me. There was very little traffic, so I started to cross the road. A few horn beeps caught my attention as I ran in front of a taxi. He stopped and shouted at me through the window, but I carried on.

Suze began to run. I picked up my pace.

We ran down streets I didn't know, Henry was a few feet ahead of me. He was trying to stay with Suze, but at the same time, make sure I was keeping up. Suze was running much faster than I had ever seen her run.

When we were kids at school, she was always slower than me and it made her mad that I always won races on school sports days. This new turn of speed was quite surprising.

She ran across a small access road and I followed. There were more horns as I ignored the traffic just as she had. Her speed meant she was leaving me behind, but I could see her bright aura still and I knew I was on the right path.

'Henry, keep up with her!' I was already starting to get out of breath.

I saw Henry turn a corner to my left and I picked up speed. I realised we were heading further downtown. I suspected we were heading towards the homeless shanty town.

Reaching the corner I turned and saw Suze was standing still looking right at me. Henry was standing to the side, and they were having a conversation.

'Garret? That is your name?' Henry said.

In a gravelly voice, Suze answered. 'What is it to you, old man?'

'Suze?' I said as I finally reached them.

The aura around Suze flickered from the dark green that dominated to a brighter yellow. 'Jimmy?' Suze said, a little panic in her voice. 'I don't know what is happening.'

Then her face and her voice changed as the green shade took over once again.

'But I do,' said the gravelly voiced Garret from within Suze's body.

Suze-Garret then raised an arm. In the hand at the end of the arm was a jet black revolver.

'AutoTech deserved it. Especially Stanley Thomas,' Suze-Garret said. The revolver was now pointing straight at my chest.

'Who is that?' asked Henry.

Suze-Garret immediately switched aim and fired at Henry; the bullet passed straight through him harmlessly.

'Did everyone else deserve it?' I said.

I saw the gun swing back to me, but Suze-Garret didn't fire. The aura around them switched from green to yellow and back again in quick succession. It was clear that there was an internal fight for dominance taking place.

'Please, Jimmy,' said Suze's voice, 'I don't know how long I can hold him back.' Tears were rolling down her face as she spoke.

'You can't!' screamed Garret's voice. 'I like it here, and I am staying. You're just a roadblock I need to break down.'

'Let my sister go, please.'

'Please,' mocked Garret's voice. 'Why not add "with a cherry on top"? You're pathetic!'

The gun was pointing right at me again. There was only one way to stop this in my mind, so I ran forward. At the same time, Suze-Garret fired again.

I ran straight into the oncoming bullet.

11

BEGIN / AGAIN

Time slowed.

I saw the gun being raised to my chest height. I watched the finger of Suze gently squeeze the trigger. A grey cloud of smoke bloomed around the gun. The noise of the shot assaulted my ears.

And then I saw the bullet.

It was too late; I'd committed to my charge. There was no turning around.

The bullet ripped through my shoulder. I felt muscle tear and I saw Body fall away from me.

Time resumed its usual progression.

With alarming speed, Body fell at my feet as I remained standing. My attention was fully focused on Body.

'James!' I heard Henry shout.

I turned in time to see Suze-Garret running away. Looking back to Body, I could see a pool of blood forming. 'You stay with Body. I'm going after Suze.'

Henry's face was a picture of confusion as he shrugged and approached Body. In the distance I could hear sirens, probably already responding to the gunshot.

Anger swelled in me as I raced after Suze-Garret. They were a sizeable distance ahead of me, but in this form, I knew I was able to go much faster than usual.

Suze-Garret stopped at the kerb, waiting for a car to pass, and then they ran into the road. Their delay helped me to make up some of the distance, and by the time they reached the other side of the road, I'd caught up.

I lunged at Suze-Garret and tried to grab onto the spirit of Garret to rip him away from my sister. Unfortunately, Garret had expected my attack and dodged to the side. Instead of grabbing onto a ghost, I slipped through a wall into a department store warehouse.

It took me a moment to gather myself and exit through the wall by which I'd entered. Annoyingly, Suze-Garret was no-where to be seen when I re-emerged onto the street.

Standing there, turning this way and that, I felt a shudder run through me and I suddenly felt weak at my translucent knees. I realised that something must be happening to Body, and I hurriedly retraced my steps.

When I arrived to where I'd been shot, the ambulance crew were already loading a trolley into the back. On the trolley was Body. I couldn't see Henry anywhere.

'Henry?' I called out. My voice was weak and shrill.

I raced to get into the ambulance before it left and, more importantly, stranded me in the middle of downtown Orlando. It was getting difficult to move; the air felt like sludge.

The doors of the ambulance were slammed shut. The thud of each door echoed in my ears. Desperation started to kick in.

The engine and sirens were turned on along with the lights. I was desperate to make it in time.

My hand reached through the back door, into the leaving ambulance, and then it was gone. Without me.

I felt another shudder and I fell to the floor, exhausted.

With every effort of my soul, I followed in the wake of the ambulance. When I concentrated, I realised there was an ethereal, silver filament floating in the air before me. One end was attached to me, somewhere in my chest, and the other end was connected to who knows where.

Trudging, struggling along, I prayed that the other end was attached to Body. I used the filament as a ghostly GPS tracker, and put all my hopes into it.

When I turned the corner and saw the lights of ORMC up ahead, my heart lifted. With a renewed sense of vigour, I pushed on. It took everything I had, but I wasn't going to stop now.

The air still felt solid as I entered the ORMC reception area. The filament went through the back wall and up one, two levels.

Through a curtain in the ER department, I finally saw Body. It was hooked up to monitors and there were two doctors, a woman and a man, standing at the side looking over a chart. The heart monitor was slowly beeping.

When I cautiously approached, Henry emerged from within Body.

'James! Thank the fates you made it. I've been keeping Body going. They think "you're" in shock.' Henry gestured to the doctors. 'You look awful.'

'Thanks,' I wheezed.

Without waiting for an invitation, I entered Body. Immediately the heart rate monitor jumped up to a normal rhythm.

'Mr. Jones?' the woman doctor to my left said.

I slowly opened my eyes. 'Call me Jimmy,' I croaked.

'What the hell!' said the other doctor. 'You're one tough fighter. We've repaired the injury to your shoulder, the bullet nearly went all the way through. Thankfully, nothing too serious was in the way. It got lodged along the edge of your shoulder blade. Honestly, we thought you also had a head injury because you were not responding.'

'Until now,' said the first doctor, 'I'm Doctor Park,' she said. 'I'm an Attending Physician here and I did the surgery on your shoulder. You're very lucky. This is my intern, Young.'

'Thank you. Could I have a drink?' My throat felt as if it were filled with razor blades as I spoke and spluttered my request.

'Of course,' said Young. He fussed about getting a cup of water and then helped me to take a sip. 'Take it slow.'

'It looks like you've recently had some surgery, Jimmy,' said Park.

'I was in a crash before I came over from the UK,' I said through more coughing. 'I'm here to try and find my sister.'

I didn't want to reveal it was Suze that shot me. In reality, it wasn't, it was the spirit dominating her body, but I guessed they wouldn't understand. I struggled with the idea myself, there was no telling what a medical practitioner would think if I told them.

For two days I drifted in an out of sleep. I thought this was either down to the fact that I'd not really slept well since arriving in Orlando, or the fact I'd had to work really hard following the filament between me and Body. Predictably, the doctors said it was the surgery and the anaesthesia.

Henry had been out and about trying to find Suze, and mostly failing. There were clues, he said, and he was getting help from Amos and Darryl, but they'd not seen her since.

I'd not seen Henry much, obviously, but now I was awake, he seemed paler and not quite himself.

The police had already spoken to me, immediately after my surgery when I'd woken up Body, I don't recall that meeting at all. This morning, Dr. Parks had told me that Lieutenant Roth was waiting to speak to me when I was ready, I told her that they could allow them in. Through the open door of my room, I could see Roth talking to Dr. Parks.

'Here they come,' said Henry. I'd not realised he was near.

Roth and Edmonds walked in to my room.

'Can we have a few minutes, Mr. Jones?' said Roth. Edmonds held back looking uncomfortable.

'Come to arrest me for being shot?' I glared at Edmonds who would not look me in the face.

'Mr. Jones, do you know who this is?' Roth held up a photo. It was a man entering the unblemished conference centre.

'That's the unconscious man we pulled from the rubble,' Henry said.

I tried not to react. 'I don't recall seeing him. Ever. Who is he?'

The picture was still being held up and in the background I could see Suze greeting attendees. She was about four feet away from the man.

'His name is Bernard Garret. He's a low level crim who usually does odd jobs for a bit of money,' Edmonds said, joining in with the conversation.

'We found a gun near to where you were shot. The type of gun is consistent with what we know Garret carries, and the ballistics match the one taken out of your shoulder,' Roth said.

'Well, at least we know who did it then. Have you arrested him yet?' I knew he was in the same hospital, but I tried to keep my best poker face.

'Thing is, he's in here. Has been for a few days,' Edmonds said. A smug grin was beginning to form on his face. 'Looks like the shooter wore gloves though because there are no prints.'

Dr. Parks was against me discharging myself, but she couldn't force me to stay. With my arm in a sling, antibiotics in my pocket, I left the hospital. Henry agreed with the good doctor, but I'd spent enough time in hospitals for a life time. I'd signed all the papers they put before me, there was definitely a large bill heading my way at some point in the future.

Outside I saw the detective Roth had assigned to follow me, she was sitting in her car pretending to not see me, so I headed over. Henry followed, not saying much.

Immediately, I saw the detective fluster with a coffee cup. When I reached the driver's door I saw she was mopping up her spilled drink.

I rapped my knuckles on the glass, making her jump again.

'If you're going to stalk me, we may as well travel together,' I said.

Her face was redder than I thought possible with embarrassment, but she reached over to the passenger seat, clearing away all papers she had there and she put them on the floor behind the driver's seat. I went around and climbed in.

'I was going to go to my sister's. I assume you know where that is?' I said with a bright smile.

'I'm not a taxi service, Jones! But I will take you,' she replied. 'What's your name?'

'Lopez.' She stared straight ahead as she drove.

'Nice to meet you Detective Lopez. And please, call me Jimmy. All my friends do.'

'Well played,' said Henry from the back seat. His voice sounded weaker than I remembered.

'I hope you're not thinking of leaving the country,' said Lopez.

'Am I not allowed to do that? I'm not a suspect in anything, I don't think you'd have any grounds to stop me.' Unlike Lopez, I kept my tone light and conversational.

'No, but you're a key witness.' Lopez had changed her tone to be a little softer, but still kept a professional air.

'Ask if she was following the night you were shot,' Henry said.

'Have you been following me this whole time?' I asked.

Lopez caught on quick. 'I wasn't following you on the night you were shot, if that's what you're fishing for.'

We rode the rest of the journey, around ten minutes, in silence. I got the impression that Lopez wasn't the chatty type. Until, that is, she pulled up outside my sister's apartment building.

'I'll take you to the airport, if that's where you're going next,' she said with a friendly tone.

'Thank you. I have a few things to do before I can go home. New friends to say goodbyes to, and all that,' I said.

Lopez just looked at me with no expression.

'You'd do well at poker with that stare,' I said with a nervous chuckle.

After another awkward pause, I nodded and closed the car door and walked away. A moment later I heard the car drive away.

'Henry, time to go back to the conference centre.' I looked for Henry, but he wasn't around.

I couldn't see him in Lopez's car that was stopped at the red light at the junction.

'Henry!'

12

KEEPER / ALONE

For the first time in weeks, Henry was no where to be seen. In a mild panic, I rushed into the elevator and furiously pressed the button for my floor.

'Henry!?' I shouted as I entered the apartment. Unexpected tears were starting to form at the corners of my eyes.

As I ran into my bedroom, my shoulder began to ache with my scurrying. Henry wasn't there either. My mind raced, trying to think of where he could be. He'd been with me all morning, warning me about leaving hospital too early. He was even with me in the car with Lopez. At least in the beginning.

Now I felt lost. Like a part of me had died.

I decided that I should find Amos, I thought he may be able to help me.

Back out on the street, with a clean hoodie on, one without a bullet hole, I called over a passing taxi.

'Where to?' asked the driver.

'The conference centre, please.' I winced a couple of times as I struggled to get my seatbelt fastened. Pain shot through my injury each time I reached over to try and clip it in.

Initially, the driver was a little wary about taking me there. I think the way I struggled with the seatbelt made him think I needed a hospital rather than a trip to a broken down building. When I said there were friends I was meeting he shrugged and set off.

At the centre, I saw there was a large crowd and News vans once again. I spotted the "News Pulse 7" crew and headed over. Approaching them I saw Harris on top of the van aiming a camera into the crowd. Jack and Greta were holding hands by the van. Then I saw Nolan, and he saw me. Immediately, he rushed over.

'Hey, Jimmy! What the hell happened?' Nolan said when he stopped at my side and tried to see if I needed assistance. He was looking at my sling, concern etched his face.

'Nothing much. My sister shot me and ran off into the night.'

'She shot you? When? Shouldn't you be resting?'

Jack, with Greta in tow, had followed Nolan and both of them now also looked at me with questioning faces.

'It's complicated, but I don't think she was in control of her actions,' I said.

All three of them then looked at me as if I was suddenly revealed as an alien with three heads.

'I'll explain,' I continued, 'but you'll not believe me. Before that, though, what's going on here?'

'A memorial service,' Jack said.

'The new mayor is showing her face,' Greta added, her tone exposed her true feelings on the mayor.

On a makeshift stage, the mic in front of the mayor whistled as she prepared to speak, and then she gave a cookie cutter style speech. She touched on the impact to families, how the city was going to rebuild and what she personally was going to do. She ended with a prayer before being bundled into a limo by her staff and driven away.

Whilst the mayor had been talking, I'd scanned the crowd. There were a handful of ghosts scattered through with the living. Some were hovering close to those who appeared to be their loved ones. Others were standing apart. I also saw Lopez, who'd nodded a friendly smile and then moved away into the midst of the crowd again.

Amos spotted me and headed over. 'It's good to see you. I heard from Henry what happened to you, but I've not seen him in a day or two.'

'I'm worried about him,' I said quietly.

Nolan and Jack both turned to me. 'Worried about who?' Jack said.

'His friend, Henry,' said Greta.

It was my turn to be surprised. All four of us, me, Nolan, Jack and Amos, looked at Greta with questions unspoken.

'You're the Way Keeper I've been hearing so much about, aren't you?' Greta asked.

'Let's go to the diner,' I said.

On the way through the quickly thinning crowd, Sara saw me and Jack and came over to join us. We continued to the diner and found a booth. Marie, the friendly waitress, poured coffee for all but Amos, who she obviously couldn't see.

I gave my new friends the potted history of my life for the last few weeks. I told them of Henry and how he had become a significant part of my life. After telling them the whole story, saying that Amos was standing by my side was easier than expected. Only Sara flinched when I said where he was, everyone else just looked at me.

It looked like they were all believing me, until Sara spoke.

'You're saying that your "nose" was actually a friendly ghost, called Henry, that went hunting through the rubble,' said Sara. She was almost upset that I didn't actually have magical powers.

'Exactly that. And now I've apparently lost him,' I said.

'Henry Costa, you said?' Nolan asked. I could feel the incredulity coming off him in waves. 'The Ghost Buster?' He laughed.

'You've heard of him?' Jack asked.

'He died in the eighties, before my time, but I'm a newshound and a bit of a ghost aficionado. So, yes, I've heard of Henry. He debunked hundreds of ghosts stories all over the world.' Nolan paused to take a drink. I could tell he was not sure what to make of my story.

'Before your scepticism gets the better of you, Nolan, I never heard him mention the name "Henry" until we sat here. However, I did hear Amos say that name outside,' Greta said. Her eyes were drilling laser holes into Nolan who threw his hands up in surrender.

Greta then looked right at Amos and nodded. Amos smiled back.

'Why did your sister shoot you?' said a familiar voice from an adjacent booth.

I turned and was not surprised to see Lopez. I hadn't seen her enter the diner, she was clearly skilled at the stealth element needed to follow someone without being obvious.

'I think the guy that caused all this chaos is possessing her.' I paused to take in the sceptical looks everyone, except Amos, was giving me. 'Whenever I've seen her, she has two auras. All people appear to me now with an aura, especially ghosts. This particular ghost is called Garret, and he has a dark green aura. I think Suze's aura is a pale yellow. My sister is showing both colours whenever I look at her, everyone else I look at only has one.' I paused as I looked about the group, looking for more looks of disbelief. My friends all looked rapt, hanging on my every word.

After a sip of coffee, I continued. 'From what I can tell, it appears Garret has taken some issue with the CEO of AutoTech,' I said.

'The car accessory guy?' asked Greta.

'It's circumstantial, but that could be motivation,' Lopez chipped in. 'The CEO has had some shady donors for his latest designs, or so the rumours go.'

'Do we know how he is, this CEO?' I asked.

'Yes,' Nolan replied. His tone implied he was coming round to my story. 'He wasn't in Orlando at the time of the explosion. Stanley Thomas was in Europe, Paris I believe, and he was due to give a keynote from his private jet on the way home. The keynote was scheduled for the end of day one, but it never happened as the explosion took place in the morning.'

'Garret clearly didn't know the plan of events,' added Greta.

'Lopez, what has the investigation turned up about Garret?' I asked.

'I can't give any details, but he has been identified as a person of interest. I will look at links between Garret and Thomas, it helps that we have even a small motivation for what happened,' Lopez said.

'Excellent. Thanks. Hopefully that will mean Roth stops looking at me for this,' I said. 'Nolan, can you find out who this Garret is? Get the scoop on the whole thing?'

'I like the idea,' Lopez said as she stood to leave, 'but I must urge you to stay out of an active police investigation.'

'I will share everything I find with you,' Nolan said as he also stood to leave. 'Jimmy, hopefully we'll get to the bottom of this and then we can have that interview.'

Greta and Jack stood next. 'I go wherever she goes,' Jack said, 'and she goes wherever Nolan goes.'

I shook Jack's hand and smiled at the enigmatic Greta as they followed Nolan out of the diner. I saw Nolan stop to talk to Marie the waitress and hand her some cash.

Sara and Amos were the only ones left. Amos was standing next to me and Sara moved to sit opposite me.

Sara took my hand, looked around as if to confirm we were alone, she couldn't see Amos, then she looked straight at me and spoke. 'I don't know exactly what is going on, nor that I fully believe you right now, but I want to help if I can. Suze was, is, a good friend, and I think I want to get to know you a lot more. If there is anything I can do, I will do it.'

'Thanks,' I said as I returned the tight squeeze on my hand.

'I will see if I can find Henry,' said Amos. 'I will leave you with your friend.'

'That would be fantastic if you could find him, Amos,' I replied as I turned to look at him. Sara gave me a questioning look as I spoke to the thin air to my side, but she didn't let go of my hand. 'I'll either be here or at my sister's place. Let me know what you find.'

Sara and I approached Marie as we headed out to leave the diner; Sara had still not let go of my hand.

'How much do I owe you, Marie?'

'Nothing. Your friend paid already,' she said. She then patted her pocket and smiled at the two of us.

The image of Nolan handing over cash dominated my memory. 'I'll have to pay him back. Thank you, Marie. I hope to be back soon.' I then left with Sara close by my side.

'Where to first?' Sara said.

'Do you have a manifest of the exhibiting companies for the show? And a list of delegates?'

13

Unlucky / For Some

In Sara's car, we drove to her office because it was only a few minutes away. She knew all the ways around the heaviest traffic, which included some areas that didn't look like you would want to stick around too long.

In the office she shared with Suze, Sara was sifting through the content of a file she had on her desk looking for the show manifest. After a minute or so, she produced the sheet with a flourish.

'What are you hoping to find?' Sara asked.

I scanned the sheet for a moment before answering. 'There. AutoTech's delegate for the conference is Andrew Jackson, and there is a number to contact him. Maybe he will have some information on where we may find Garret.'

Sara was already dialling the number before I finished speaking. The phone rang three, four times before being answered by a man's gruff voice. Sara put the call onto speaker so I could hear too.

'Hi, this is Andrew Jackson, how can I help?' said the raspy voice.

'Mr. Jackson, I am Sara Snow from Snow Events Management. I'm calling you with regards to the recent technology expo that should have taken place here in Orlando.'

'The one where the place exploded?' Jackson almost whispered.

'Yes,' I said. 'My name is Jimmy Jones, and I wonder if you could help me.'

'I couldn't make the conference, I've been ill. I was replaced by a colleague, Bianca West, so I don't think there is much I could do to help. I think poor Bianca is still in the hospital,' said Jackson.

'Hopefully she is getting all the treatment she needs,' I said. I looked at Sara who waved her hand at me, urging me to continue. 'However, I need some help locating someone you may have worked with. A Bernard Garret.'

'I already spoke to the police about that psycho.' Jackson coughed as he spoke.

'He shot me two days ago, and I need to find him because I think he knows where my sister is.'

'He shot you? I knew he wasn't sane. He started to go on long rants about the government being evil and a number of other crazy ideas. This was right after his mom was admitted to hospital.'

'Do you know her name?' Sara asked.

'Celia or Cecilia, I believe. He's probably visiting her if he's not on the street already. Sorry, I have to go,' Jackson paused for a few more coughs, 'talking is taking a lot of effort.'

'No problem, thanks for your time,' said Sara.

'Hope you find your sister,' Jackson spluttered as he ended the call.

'Back to hospital it is then,' I said.

Another quick trip in her car later and we were walking into the hospital reception.

Dr. Parks was walking through the reception area when we arrived. 'Hi Jimmy, is everything OK?' she said before I had a chance to speak.

'Hello, this is my friend, Sara. I'm fine. It aches a fair amount, but I'm good for now. I'm still trying to find my sister, and I think there may well be a clue here. And possibly something that may help understand what happened to me,' I said.

'Here?' Parks said.

'We believe that Garret, the man who shot me, admitted his mother here a short while ago,' I said.

'How does that help?' the doctor asked. 'Isn't he actually in a coma here already? I can't see how he would have shot you.'

'It's complicated. I can separate myself, my spiritual and physical selves.' I saw Parks' face contort into a million questions. 'Yeah, I know. I sound crazy. I just need to know where Celia or Cecilia Garret is and I will hopefully find my sister.'

'I can't tell you details of a patient you're not related to, that is against hospital policy.' Parks looked at me sternly.

'You don't need to tell me anything. I will physically stay right here.' I emphatically pointed to the floor at my feet. 'You can go over the other side of the desk over there, look up her location and never even say a word.' I smiled.

'Honestly, you won't need to speak. You won't break any rules,' added Sara.

Confused, but intrigued, Parks went over to the desk. 'This one?' she asked.

I nodded, and then I immediately separated from Body. I heard Sara gasp as Body's face went slack and his shoulders slumped a little, but he just stood there. I rushed over to where Parks was stood and slid straight through the desk to look at the computer screen over Parks' shoulder.

Sara was fussing over Body, trying to make sure he was alright. Parks was looking intently at Sara and Body.

Move your arm. Tell Parks to start, I messaged Body.

Body raised his good hand and waved to Parks. The doctor shrugged and began her search. Her fingers flew over the keys and she quickly located the record of a Cecelia Garret. Next to her name I saw the floor and room where she was being treated and the name of the doctor treating her. Quickly, I sped back into Body.

Sara saw the immediate change in my outward appearance and I smiled to her. Parks came back over and looked at me with curious eyes.

'Thanks. Looks like a neuro doctor called Nichols is looking after Mrs. Garret on the third floor,' I said.

The look of shock on both Parks' and Sara's face made me laugh a little. I shrugged as if to say "told you".

'How did you get that information?'

'Told you, I can separate. We need to get moving,' I said to Sara. 'They are thinking of moving her to a care home. Garret's family have decided to take her out of hospital.'

'Go,' said Sara.

I knew immediately that she meant I should leave Body and go looking. Without another word I separated from Body again and set off through the walls and floors heading for the room number I'd seen on screen.

Body, stay with Sara, I thought to my physical self as I flew away.

I sped through to where I thought Mrs. Garret was being treated and I immediately saw Suze. She had not spotted me, she was staring through the window into a room where there were a few people gathered.

Concentrating on Suze, there was something different. The dark green aura looked stronger than I'd seen it before. It was clear that the dark green aura was winning. The yellow aura was much smaller than the dark green.

'Suze!' I shouted.

Not one living person turned to look at me, apart from Suze. I saw tears streaking her face, but I also saw the eyes of evil.

'I'm going to kill you for good this time,' Suze-Garret hissed.

I didn't give Suze-Garret time to react, I rushed towards my sister.

14

— · —

TIME / TO LEAVE

I flew right at my sister, I wanted to grab hold of Garret by his ghostly throat.

Suze-Garret didn't react fast enough and I joined both Suze and Garret in a dark, shadowy place. There was a thick mist covering the ethereal ground that I could feel, but not see, beneath my feet.

'Jimmy?' Suze said in surprise. She reached over to me, but the dark shape of Garret stepped between us.

'Little Jimmy has come to save his sister. What a joke!' His voice echoed off invisible walls.

Garret's size increased twofold, and I saw Suze cowering on the floor behind him. He'd become translucent and in this environment I didn't expect to see through another spirit. I thought we'd be solid, whole.

I lunged for Garret and my fist connected with his chin.

Through Suze's eyes, I could see visions, flashes really. It appeared that Suze was falling, and medics were rushing to help her. My punch on Garret's spirit had an effect on Suze's physical self. Suze's eyes fluttered shut as she passed out.

Garret roared and rushed back at me with fists flying. I ducked and dodged, but one out of every three punches still found their mark.

On the floor, Suze was unconscious and looking weak. I needed to get Garret to follow me and leave Suze.

Throwing a few punches of my own, I heard Garret laughing.

'You've not done this before. Have you, Little Jimmy?' Garret towered above me as he increased his own size again.

He was right. I'd avoided fights all my life; never even taken self defence classes. However, I tried to channel Jet Li and Jackie Chan, and whoever else I could remember, from all the martial arts movies I'd watched over the years.

Another of my punches connected with Garret and I saw I'd created a tear through his stretched out spirit.

Garret shuddered with the effort of maintaining his size. In response, I raged and threw a flurry of punches. A number of them successfully hit, and I caused more damage to his spirit form.

'If you want to kill me, you're going to have to hit me first,' I taunted.

There was a lurch to the floor and the mist cleared a little. Suze was now fully visible, but she didn't move. Another lurch, and I recognised the sound coming through Suze's ears. Garret was coated in an electrical cloud as the defibrillator sent a shower of sparks throughout Suze's body.

'You see that? That means it's time to leave. Suze is dead, and they're trying to revive her,' I said. 'If you want me, come get me!'

I rushed out of Suze's body just before another shock from the defibrillator hit. A moment later, Garret burst out of her body too.

'I'm going to enjoy this!' Garret screamed.

Before he could lunge at me, he was pulled backwards.

'Oh, I remember this part,' I said.

Garret was pulled again; much further away from me this time.

'Suze is not the only one being shocked, by the looks. Your body is dying, and they're trying to revive you too.' I smirked.

'No!' Garret shouted.

'Oh yes. And this time you've got no choice.' I followed as Garret was pulled faster towards his body. 'I'll be waiting for you.'

He was pulled right into his body, and I saw him take a breath as he took up residence back where he belonged.

Weakness overtook me as it had when I'd lost Body in the ambulance. I fell to my knees. Looking around, I saw the silver filament connecting me to Body. I followed it as fast as I could. Slipping through floors and walls, people and equipment, I tried to get back as soon as possible.

Body wasn't in reception as I was expecting, but on a gurney in the emergency room. Sara was standing by Body's side, worry showed on her face.

Sit up, Body, I said in my mind.

Immediately, Body responded. The medics and Sara all stepped back a little.

'Jimmy?' Sara said.

With effort I climbed back into Body and looked about at the shocked faces about me, all staring with confusion.

'I'm fine. I'm fine,' I said.

Parks placed her stethoscope around her neck. 'Mr. Jones, what was that? Do you have a history of neurological complaints?'

'No. I told you, I can separate myself.' I swung my legs to the side and stood. Then I turned to Sara. 'Garret's back in his own skin, but now I need to get to Suze.'

'She's here?' Sara asked.

'Doctor, I need to go to my sister. She's in trouble. Last I saw she was being shocked because her heart had stopped. I don't know if they're going to be able to identify her, she may not have anything on her other than the clothes on her back.'

Parks worked her magic on the hospital computers again and agreed to help me find Suze. I confirmed to the hospital who she was, and tried to give details of her medical history. What I remembered at least.

The doctor looking after her, a Philip Liang, told me they didn't know when Suze would wake up, but she was otherwise fine. He mentioned something about potential brain damage, but couldn't tell me more at this stage. Suze was not on a ventilator, which the doctor said could only be a good thing.

Sara had to practically force me to leave the hospital. Dr. Parks was worried I wasn't getting enough rest and Dr. Liang said there was nothing I could do but wait. With a heavy heart, I allowed Sara to take me home.

At Suze's apartment, Sara helped me into the bedroom. I could barely move and I flopped, with an accompanying howl of pain from my shoulder, onto my bed. Sara pulled off my shoes before covering me with a woollen blanket. I was exhausted and sleep found me quickly. I don't recall her turning off the bedroom light.

When the morning light broke through the window, I was ready to wake. I could hear movement coming from the kitchen. The clink of plates and pans and the smell of bacon roused me from my bed.

Following my nose, I found Sara cooking breakfast.

'Good morning, sleepyhead,' Sara said. She placed a plate of bacon and eggs before me. 'Hope you're not vegetarian.'

'Looks good,' I said and I started on the bacon.

Sara's phone rang while I ate. She put the phone on the counter and turned on speakerphone.

'Hi, Jack,' said Sara.

'Hey, I'm here with Nolan,' said Jack.

'Hi,' said Nolan. 'We've got some info about this Garret. Apparently he was laid off from AutoTech. He was accused, but there was no proof, of embezzlement.'

'Well, he's not going anywhere. Last I saw of him was in the hospital. We found my sister, she is in hospital too. She's unconscious, but alive,' I said.

'Hey, Jimmy. That's good news,' Jack didn't sound surprised to hear my voice this early in the day on Sara's phone.

The door intercom behind me buzzed, making me jump slightly.

'Hello,' I tentatively said into the receiver.

'Hi. It's Lopez. Can I come up?'

I buzzed her through and a moment or two later, she was knocking on the door to the apartment. Sara and I had said bye to Jack and Nolan for the time being.

'Come in,' I said.

'I'm glad you're safe. I've just come from the hospital where we had some trouble. Garret woke, he fought his doctors, injuring a few and is now missing. There's one doctor, a general surgeon by the name of Parks, who is currently fighting for her life. She was apparently attacked by Garret in his escape,' said Lopez.

'What about Suze?' I couldn't hide the worry in my voice.

'She is safe. We don't think she's at risk, but Roth has an officer to the floor to look after her.'

Sara grabbed my arm.

'I need to see her,' I said.

'I'll take you,' said Lopez. 'We found that Garret has sent a number of threatening emails to Stanley Thomas and even had to be escorted off the premises of AutoTech after his employment was terminated.' Lopez looked at me with concern.

'Garret is missing?' asked Sara.

Lopez's phone started to ring before she could answer.

15

REUNITED / AT LAST

Lopez looked at her phone, confused. 'Lieutenant?' she said when she answered. Her voice was flat, and she didn't look at either myself or Sara while speaking to the Lieutenant.

Thoughts of my sister were running through my imagination, which centred on what Garret could have done to her.

'There's something happening at the hospital,' said Lopez when she'd finished the call with Roth.

Lopez was ordered to the hospital, and I insisted on going with her. Sara too. On the drive, I watched Lopez. Her demeanour had changed from the first time we'd met, but I couldn't figure out quite what.

The detective's purple aura had little flashes of white, which worked in harmony with the purple. There was no fight for dominance here.

'Henry?' I said.

Lopez turned to me and smiled; it was the first time I'd seen her do this.

'Hello, James.' It was Henry's voice with Lopez's face looking at me. 'I was fading away. There was "a light", there still is.

However, I am not ready. We started this together, and I aim to finish it together.'

'What about Lopez?' I asked.

'I'm here too. This is quite disturbing,' Lopez replied.

'We're working together, with the good detective's permission, of course. When you left the hospital, I thought I was going to disappear, but I couldn't let you down,' said Henry.

It was confusing to hear them both speak from one mouth, but I was really happy to be able to talk to my friend again.

'Why didn't you say anything before? At the diner?' I asked.

Henry chuckled. 'I wasn't strong enough. At first, I didn't know how to be, well, myself, inside a physical body again. However, we came to an agreement, the detective and I, and here I am.'

'We're at the hospital,' said Lopez.

We pulled in through the entrance to the hospital and saw a large number of police cars gathered there.

'There's Roth,' said Lopez.

Standing with a car between her and the entrance doors, Roth was giving out tasks. Edmonds led two other officers to the south.

'Please stay back,' Roth said when I got out of the car.

'What's happening?' Sara said.

'It's Garret,' I said.

Roth didn't confirm my guess. 'Lopez, take a couple of uniforms and go for the east door. Edmonds has gone for the south.'

'Go get her. Make her safe,' Sara said. She was looking straight into my eyes, and without missing a beat she addressed Roth. 'Lieutenant, can you help me catch Jimmy.'

I smiled at her, and then I surprised myself by kissing Sara. She kissed me back, passionately. I wanted that kiss to last forever, but I knew forever had to wait. Lifting my head and looking at her again, I gave her another smile and then leapt out of Body.

As I flew towards the hospital doors, I heard Roth shout for a medic. Over my shoulder, I saw Body slump into Sara's arms as Roth was running over to help.

Passing unhindered through the doors, I saw chains wrapped tightly, and padlocked, around the inside door handles. There were wires running from the chains to plastic bottles containing liquid that smelled of oil, or petrol.

After a brief look around, I carried on up through the ceiling. Up another floor, and then I headed through room after room. I saw some nurses hiding under a counter and I wished I could help them. Unfortunately, they couldn't see me and there was nothing I could do. With the doors rigged, there was no easy way out.

'Henry, where are you when I need you?'

'I'm right here, James,' Henry said from behind.

'Henry?'

'What's the plan?' Henry's form flickered as he spoke.

'I'm not sure yet. Winging it a little here. Are you okay?' I asked.

'Of course.' Henry smiled. 'Let's find this guy.'

Henry shot ahead, and I followed. He was almost completely transparent, which worried me, but I was glad he was here.

'You have to pull him out of his body, I'm not strong enough for that. Once you have him, I'll take him to the after,' said Henry.

'What? No! I'll do that.'

'I've been dead longer than I was alive. It's my time. I've seen the light, or so they say.' Henry stopped and turned around. His smile was brighter than his aura, and I could see he was happier than I'd ever seen before.

'But-' I started to say.

'I've enjoyed having a friend again, but we don't have time for sentiment right now. I believe your sister's room is around this corner. Ready?'

Resigned, I nodded and then I floated around the corner to see Garret standing over my sister. Suze was unconscious and propped up against the bed, her hands and feet were tied with bandages.

Garret was speaking on the phone. 'Bring me that idiot who fired me, and I'll let all the hostages go.'

'Hostages?' I said quietly as I looked about.

In a side room, all tied together, I saw a police officer and around eight or nine nurses and doctors. They were all unconscious, like Suze, and I also saw the door to their room was chained shut.

'Garret!' I shouted. I didn't expect him to hear me, but he did.

'You!' he stammered. He dropped the phone, which shattered on the hard floor at his feet.

Garret then raised his free hand, which held a gun that he immediately fired in my direction. The bullet sailed right through my forehead without causing any harm.

'Are you really that stupid? You already shot me once. If it didn't stop me then, it isn't going to now,' I said.

Suze squirmed, catching Garret's attention. 'Stupid, eh?' He then pointed his gun at Suze's chest.

Time slowed again for me. I could see Garret's finger closing on the trigger. He was staring right at me, smirking with all the evil he could muster.

I charged at Garret, my arms out in a classic Superman pose in mid-flight.

The surprise on Garret's face made me slightly giddy, and I sped on.

My hands connected with his spirit, my fingers wrapped around his throat. I carried him on and out of his body with my momentum. He was punching and scratching at me to make me let go.

Behind me, his physical self slumped forward, face-planting into the hard floor. The gun scattered under a chair.

'This time there's no defibrillator,' I said and I threw him away like a rag doll.

I flew at him again and my taunt was quickly followed with a punch to his chin, and another to his gut. Our ghostly forms were connecting like physical bodies.

Behind Garret, Henry waited. I saw his aura getting brighter; Garret hadn't seen him. Henry's arms were out wide, waiting to grapple with Garret. To push him in the right direction, I threw a few wild punches. Garret easily dodged my swinging arms, and even laughed a little.

'You need the gym, Little Jimmy. This isn't your thing. Is it?' Garret said as he threw punches of his own, forcing me backwards.

Even being a ghost, getting punched in the jaw hurt like hell. Two, then three of Garret's blows later and I bellowed like an angry bear. With a fire in me I never knew I had, I charged at Garret again.

I wrapped my arms around Garret's middle, and kept on roaring and pushing. When Henry was only a step or two further on, Garret sensed something was going on. He tried to push me back, and I could feel him digging his elbows into my back, one after the other. I didn't care. I was taking him to the after.

'No!' screamed Garret. 'What is that light?'

Garret's fury intensified. His fists were repeatedly slamming into my back with a scary speed, but I was determined.

One more step, and we were engulfed in Henry's white light.

We both tumbled into a white space. Garret landed a few feet away from where I stopped and he was first to his feet.

'What have you done?' Garret shouted. His voice echoed around what felt like an infinite space.

'Taken you out of the world. That's what,' I spat. In my mouth, I tasted blood.

'Time to go,' Henry said. His voice was large and booming.

'Who's here?' Garret sounded scared for the first time since I'd met him.

'It's over,' I said.

Henry loomed out of the unseen white walls and wrapped Garret in his open arms. Garret squirmed and struggled against Henry's grip.

'James, the last few months have been amazing. I really wish we could have had longer,' Henry was calm, his grasp on Garret seemed like nothing. He may as well have been holding a sleeping baby.

'I don't want you to go,' I said. 'What am I going to do without you?'

'You'll have your sister. And isn't there someone you're sweet on? The lovely Sara?' Henry was smiling, a little twinkle in his eye.

'I'm going to miss you.' Tears were rolling down my face.

'And I you,' Henry said as he faded into the white with the squirming and raging Garret.

There was a jolt and I felt the now familiar pull of a defibrillator.

'Goodbye, my friend,' Henry's voice faded into the distance.

There was another jolt, and then I heard voices around me.

'We've got a heartbeat,' said a woman to my left.

'Jimmy?' I heard Sara say.

I struggled to open my eyes, but when I did I saw Roth, Sara and two paramedics at my side. Sara pushed pass the woman to my left and grabbed my face before kissing me again.

'It's safe. Garret has died,' I croaked. 'He's up on the third floor, all the hostages are unconscious. Be careful, though, he's trapped the doors with some sort of petrol bomb.'

Immediately, Roth was on her radio, giving out more orders.

Sara would not let go of me even though the paramedics were putting me into the back of an ambulance. All around, police and medics were rushing about trying to get back into the hospital.

I woke to the gentle beeping of a heart monitor. The sun was creeping through the half drawn blinds. My blurry eyes slowly took in the room. In a chair, covered in a blue blanket, was Sara. Her eyes were closed, a little drool was running down her chin, and she was breathing lightly.

'Sara?' I said.

Her eyes shot open, and she sat up with a start. 'I'm not sleeping.' She awkwardly rubbed her damp chin with the back of her hand.

'Jimmy?!' It was Suze. She was standing in the doorway, two coffees in her hands.

I turned too quickly, and my shoulder complained with a vengeance of pain.

'Suze? It is so good to see you.' I coughed as I spoke.

'Here, you've been asleep four days. Take a sip,' Sara was at my side with a glass of water; a paper straw was poking its way out of the cup.

'I'll get a doctor,' Suze said.

'What's happened?' I asked.

'You did what was needed. Garret was found face down, dead. No one knows why, but heart attack is the likeliest cause. Your sister is safe,' Sara said.

Suze returned and grabbed my free hand.

'And you're OK too,' Sara finished.

The doctor came in, fished out a small light from his pocket and shone it in my eyes. First the left, then the right.

'Well, James, everything looks good from what we can see. I believe you can go home soon,' said the doctor. His voice sounded familiar.

'Henry?' I said.